Marlborough a
Forest

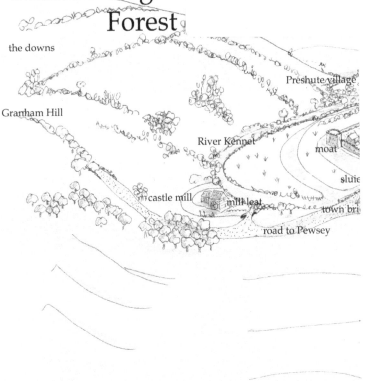

the downs

Granham Hill

Preshute village

River Kennet

moat

sluie

castle mill

mill leat

town bri

road to Pewsey

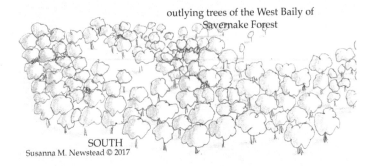

outlying trees of the West Baily of
Savernake Forest

SOUTH

Susanna M. Newstead © 2017

Marlborough Town and the forest c.1200 (2)

ton Road

stone yard

The Common

The Bu

castle

Chantry Lane

Back Lane

St. Peter's

High Street

Chandler's Yard

south field

Tiggins Lane

shoemaker's house

Ironmong Lane

Nick's house

shambles

River Kennet

Priory

Crooks Yard

High Cross

weavers

Johnan hou

west to Pewsey and Devizes

town mill

tanners

St. Mary

Oxford Stre

culverstones

The Marsh

cherry orchard

Culvermead

Wagon Yard

The Ropery

the brid

Savernake Forest

Salisbury Road

SOUTH

to scale

Susanna M. Newstead © 2017

Marlborough and the forest c. 1200 (3)

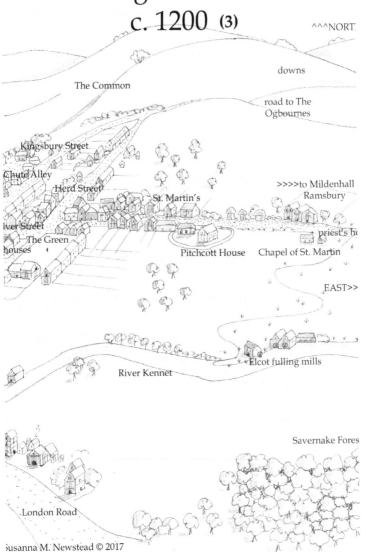

^^^NORT.

downs

road to The
Ogbournes

The Common

Kingsbury Street

Chute Alley

Herd Street

St. Martin's

>>>>to Mildenhall
Ramsbury

Iver Street

The Green

houses

priest's h

Pitchcott House

Chapel of St. Martin

EAST>>

Elcot fulling mills

River Kennet

Savernake Fores

London Road

Susanna M. Newstead © 2017

HUNTING THE WREN

The wren, the wren is king of the birds
St. Stephen's Day was caught in the furze
Although he is little his family is great
We pray you, good people to give us a treat.
Come out with the money, mister,
or else bad health we'll be singing.
We pray you, good people, to give us a treat.
"We'll hunt the wren," says Robin to Bobbin,
"We'll hunt the wren," says Richard to Robin,
"We'll hunt the wren," says Jack of the land,
"We'll hunt the wren," says everyone.
"Where oh where?" says Robin to Bobbin,
"Where oh where?" says Richard to Robin,
"Where oh where?" says Jack of the land,
"Where oh where?" says everyone.
"In yonder green bush,"
"How get him down?"
"With sticks and stones,"
"How get him home?"
"The brewer's big cart,"
"How'll we eat him?"
"With knifes and forks,"
"Who'll come to the dinner?"
"The King and the Queen,"
"Eyes to the blind,"
"Legs to the lame,"
"Luck to the poor,"
"Bones to the dogs," says everyone.

Traditional song possibly from Norfolk. Unknown date.
A St. Stephen's Day tradition. 26th December.

CHAPTER ONE ~ THE BOOK
MARLBOROUGH WILTSHIRE 1207

Master Cowper was ill. He had been ill for some time and, although he was worried, would not call upon a doctor.

Everyone knows that when you are ill, you must consult a doctor. If you can't afford one then there will be some cunning woman who might be able to help you.

If you consult a doctor, he will look at your urine and take pennies from you to tell you that you are indeed *ill*. If he is a *proper* doctor, he will draw up an astrological chart for you and that will tell him what is wrong with you and how to cure you.

If, as in this case here, your doctor will not draw up a chart, you must consult an astrologer.

Master Cowper's wife nagged him.

In order to get himself a bit of peace and quiet, Master Cowper, consulted the only astrologer in the town.

*****

The master astrologer consulted his charts.

"You are, Master Cowper, an Aquarian with a moon of Virgo."

"I am?"

"Indeed."

"And does that mean that the ….difficulty I am having…is…"

"No, no. Do not fear. It is not mortal. Unpleasant and painful, but not mortal."

"Oh...good."

"You are a sensitive soul. Your earth-sign Virgo Moon tells us that emotionally you are an extremely complicated man. You see... in order to bring a sense of clarity to your emotions you need to understand life's matters on a minute and detailed level. In fact, you have a natural talent when it comes to understanding the complex world of feelings and emotions. This makes you a good counsellor for your friends and family"

"Huh! Tell that to my wife. She never listens to me."

The astrologer chuckled.

"Well...how many times have you given her guidance and then...a little while later, you find her implementing your advice?"

Cowper's brow cleared. "You're right… it's not always immediate."

"Helping others in this way is your chosen method for showing love and affection to those close to you. However, sir, you are not prone to displays of emotions. Oh no, you are far too reserved for that!"

"Well...yes… I do tend to hold back."

"And it is the holding back which has given you this...little problem."

"Oh?"

"Yes indeed. Holding back the urine...not being able to let it go."

"Well, sometimes, I can't stop it."

"Ah yes. And there is pain is there not. In the lower back and in the... excuse me... male member?"

"Why... yes... yes there is."

"Then return to Dr. Johannes and tell him that I say that you need something to clear out the bladder. And a compound of nettle and vegetables and fruit will clear the blockage and you'll be right in no time."

"Master apothecary will make me a potion I'm sure."

"I'm sure he will. But sir, just eat more fruit whenever you can."

Cowper handed over money, feeling very pleased with himself and went to the outer door.

"Ah... and Master Copwer."

"Yes."

"Be very careful just at the moment...four wheeled objects are not your friend today. Just a convivial warning."

"Oh! Well, erm... thank you Master Celest." And he left.

Master Celest sighed. "I wish they were all so easy." He dropped the coins into his money box.

Upon the next instant there was a screeching and bellowing outside his shop and he poked his head from the door.

Master Cowper was sitting in the dust of the road, rubbing his elbow.

"Four wheels, Master Cowper!" shouted Celest, as the cart from the flour mill trundled past and along the road.

"Ah...yes..." Cowper laughed, embarrassed by his accident. "I'll take greater care...I didn't see it."

"Keep your eyes open!"

"I will." Cowper picked himself up and glared after the cart with its four oxen. "All day."

*****

In a side room, Bennet of Marlborough, Master Celest's journeyman apprentice, lifted his head and tried to work out what the noise had been.

He stretched an ear towards the window.

Oxen bellowing and a man's voice yelling expletives.

Bennet snorted. Didn't sound as if anyone was really hurt.

He went back to his charts and his mathematical analyses. The figures and little symbols swam before his eyes. He stood and stretched his arms above his head, groaning with the pleasure of the cracking muscles. He threw back his shoulders. Aw, how sore they were.

He covered over the astrological computations upon which he had been working as his master had taught him. They should not be left for prying eyes, nor open to unseen creatures and he sauntered over to the door. Once there his eyes ranged over the room behind him.

A small room with just one tiny window, a bench upon which lay parchment, ink and charcoal with which to draw and write. On the other wall another bench with his master's armillary sphere and his astrolabe; his prized possession. There too lay other equipment of his trade. Most of them covered against the dust which came through the window of the cramped room, from the street directly outside.

Thus Bennet checked everything before he exited and locked the door.

His master looked up.

"Ah... Bennet. Heard the noise did you?"

"Yessir."

"Going out for a little walk?"

"Aye, sir. The weather is warm today and it's stuffy in the back."

"And your neck is hurting again I see."

Bennet laughed. "Too much bending over calculations." He rubbed the back of his neck.

"Well then... go out and have a walk around. It doesn't do a body any good being cooped up all day."

Bennet smiled at this kind and generous man.

People were always surprised when they first met Master Geoffrey Celest. They imagined the man to be strange, perhaps ugly; a man with some odd deformity, maybe, which set him aside from normal mortals, for he was skilled in the arcane practices of astrological computations. He *must* look strange and different from other men, for he knew what the world was about, what the world was made of, what the world would DO. How could he be normal?

But Bennet knew otherwise. The man was as normal as...well...as

4

normal as...he was. It was his knowledge which was uncommon.

And then he started to think about himself. He stepped out into the street and a puff of dust kicked up by a passing mule made him sneeze. He looked out over the wide High Street. Wednesday. Market day. It was very busy.

If his master was normal, what was he? He was a journeyman astrologer and lucky to be so. That opportunity was not given to many young men. Oh, they might become coopers or masons, rope makers or butchers but astrologers? *Astrologers* had to be chosen from the educated. From those who could read and compute.

Bennet started to wander along the side of the road. He passed the cordwainer's shop. The door was open and Bennet poked his head through, "Good afternoon Mistress Cordwainer."

"Why hello young Bennet. Sorry but Harry isn't here."

"That doesn't matter. I am simply taking my ease for a while. Can you tell him I was asking after him?" He smiled and was on his way.

He passed the high wall of the Priory of St. Margaret of Antioch and thanked his stars, (and he knew them intimately,) that he was not walled up behind them. This sort of place was the first option for most educated young lads; those with no fortune, land, or prospects; the church or servitude of a sort, as a clerk. He had avoided both. He was almost twenty one and nearly out of his apprenticeship. Two more weeks and he would be a fully qualified astrologer. He smiled to himself. "I did it. I am almost there."

On he went and crossed the road at the end of the High Street disappearing into the bushes behind the newly built church of St. Peter.

There were a few blackberries on the bushes here and there and he leaned over and picked a couple, stuffing them into his mouth. Pah! They *were* juicy and black but the lack of sun had given them no sweetness. He spat them out. As he righted himself, a wren came whooshing out of the bush at speed, chattering his distress call, high pitched, angry and anguished.

Bennet crossed himself. "Sorry Master Wren." All men knew that the wren was the king of birds, the cleverest of them all. The wren had been widely acknowledged for many centuries as rather special.

Bennet knew all the folk tales associated with this diminutive bird. He knew its power. He knew its astrological meaning and he knew what happened when you annoyed a wren without apologising!

Off he went, his feet taking him to the other side of the road and the series of shops located there. The fletcher. The fleshmonger. The cutler.

He had no need to visit any of them.

Dashing back across the road and twisting around the tail of a cart upon which sat a matronly woman in dark brown and a girl in a faded red dress with a long dark plait down her back, he made for the door of his own home again.

The girl's hazel eyes followed him.

"Stop! Stop!" Shouted a voice. Bennet turned.

"Where can I find the astrologer?" said the matron, clambering down from the cart.

Bennet rushed up to help her, for she was struggling to find her feet.

"The door lies straight before you, madam," said Bennet, indicating the scruffy door with an armillary sphere crudely painted upon it in green, more bare wood than paint.

"Ah." She turned for the girl but she had already jumped down with a bounce.

"Come on Christa."

Bennet scuttled forward to open the door and bowed them through.

As he followed them, he heard the woman say, "Well that's a good start. If he belongs *here*, he has good manners."

Master Celest looked up and adjusted his round hat.

"Madam. Welcome. Do take a seat."

The woman bustled in, sat and put down her basket. The girl Christa, stood by her elbow. Bennet closed the door quietly and the

6

noise of the street faded.

"You have come to ask about your health?"

The woman's eyes grew round and huge. "How did you know that?"

The girl called Christa looked to the heavens, Bennet noted.

"Most people when they come to me are seeking help with their health. It is no surprise to me and should not be to you, dear lady."

The 'dear lady' seemed to calm the woman and she let out a huge sigh. "Ah yes. I see."

'Why is it," said Bennet to himself, 'that folk think that we know all there is to know about them before we have even taken their particulars? We are not mind readers.'

The woman leaned forward. "Margaret Basketwright, from Manton."

"I am pleased to make your acquaintance," said Celest.

The master nodded to Bennet who walked over to the trestle and picked up a piece of parchment, a pen and ink.

"Scribe, Bennet."

"Aye master."

Bennet flattened out the parchment and began to scribble. First he wrote the date, in the way in which his master had taught him.

'The day after the Kalends of July, in the sixth year of the reign of the Lord John, our King.'

Then he listened to the answers which the woman was giving to questions from Master Celest.

"And your date of birth is?"

"Oh. Date of birth? Well...I am not quite sure."

"Madam, I will be unable to help you, if you cannot tell me when you were born. Everything depends upon this. I can, if we fall at this first hurdle, try to reconstruct the day of your birth by events others might remember, though I will be unable to be really accurate with my calculations."

"Oh. Well... erm... it was an April day and my mother told me that the King...that's Henry of course, of blessed memory, had passed by on the road just before I came."

"Hmm." Master Celest put his fingers to his lips.

"Bennet, the book of the Kings."

"Yessir."

It was not really a book. One couldn't really dignify this bundle of parchments with the name 'book' but he knew what his master had meant.

It was a hotchpotch of single sheets collected together with dates and events upon it.

"And your approximate age is...?"

The woman looked offended.

"Madam I cannot help if I do not know."

"Well...I think I am about thirty three. I was married at sixteen and my eldest was born..."

"I suspect then that it was that monarch's little trip into the West Country in 1173. That would make sense."

Bennet wrote, 1173. April.

"And that was..." His master traced a finger down the list on the page. "On the very first day. The kalends."

April the first, wrote Bennet.

"And now we come to the real difficulty. I will not be able to do very much unless you can tell me at what time of the day you were born." He looked up hopefully.

"Ah," said the woman.

"The Lord King passed through the town at just a scrape after midday, sir," said Bennet. "Riding fast as usual."

"Ah yes, I had forgotten you have learned this book off by heart, haven't you?"

Celest chuckled. "He has a prodigious memory, my journeyman, though he's soon to be a fully-fledged astrologer himself."

Bennet threw a glance in the direction of the girl who looked impressed.

"So at Manton we can expect the time to have been a little before midday."

"So write that down Bennet."

"Yes master."

"Read it back to me."

"Margaret Basketwright of Manton born April 1st at just before midday in the year of our lord, 1173."

"Well...that should not be difficult."

"So you *can* help me?"

"I can indeed. I will calculate your chart and if you can come back in a week we will have an answer for you."

"A week?"

"It will take us a while to do it. And meanwhile we have other things we must be doing."

"The master will not just be working for you, madam," said Bennet with a sweet smile. "He is much in demand in the town and county."

"A week...oh..."

The young girl now came forward. "Sir. Madam is much troubled by her pains. She wishes to know what they are and how she might cure them."

"Then speak to a doctor."

"Doctor! Pah. I do not trust doctors," said Margaret dismissively.

"Doctor Johannes is a capital fellow."

"Well maybe he is to *you*...but."

"When we have calculated your horoscope, we will require you to take it to Doctor Johannes and he will interpret it medically and advise you accordingly."

"I can't stand the pains much longer."

The girl put her hand lovingly on Mistress Basketwright's arm. "Madam, you have put up with it these six months. One more week...?"

"Oh I suppose so."

"Where do you dwell, mistress?"

"Manton, at the first cottage behind the grange."

If we manage to cast your horoscope before next week, Bennet will come to you with an explanation."

"Your lad?"

The girl Christa smiled and then downed her eyes quickly.

"He is no lad. He is twenty one in a few weeks. And a master astrologer as good as me. In fact he will be the one to cast it for you. I will be unable."

Bennet looked up puzzled.

"Very well then."

The master astrologer told the woman how much the consultation would cost.

"How much?"

"There are hours of work in this madam. Hours and much special knowledge. This cannot come cheap."

Margaret Basketwright tutted and reached into her purse.

"Oh this had better be worth it."

"I promise you, madam, said Bennet rising and walking to the door, "Master Celest never fails. He is the best astrologer this side of London."

The woman sniffed and ducked through the door.

Christa gently closed it after her and smiled sweetly with a thank you.

Master Geoffrey Celest wiped his forehead. "I am a little fatigued, Bennet."

"Then sir, go and lie down upstairs."

"Aye...I will...I will."

"I will begin the chart for Mistress Partridge and her new buildings."

"Yes. Yes, that would be a good use of your time." The man stood and Bennet helped him to the stairs.

He was looking his age, thought Bennet. He was well over sixty and tired easily now. Perhaps it was a good thing that he was coming out of his apprenticeship soon for he could take over the hard work from Master Geoffrey, leaving him more time to take his ease.

He would be happy to do that. Bennet was very fond of his old master.

"Take some money from the box, Ben and go and get some of Mistress Alice Brewster's ale, if you will. I think you'll feel in need of something good, later."

"I'll bring it straight back," said Bennet looking in concern at his master. "You will be alright?"

"I will. I'll be upstairs lying down." He heaved himself up the narrow and steep stairs and Bennet heard the ropes of the man's bed creak as he lay down.

*****

When he returned and took the jug upstairs to their private quarters, Master Geoffrey was fast asleep.

'I'll leave him to sleep and he can have the ale later,' he told himself.

He went down to the work room, locked the outer door and fetched his parchment upstairs so that he could work by the light of the upper windows and be close by should his master need him.

He laid out the tools of his trade.

His Ptolemy's Tetrabiblos was getting a little tatty now, he had consulted it so often and it had already been somewhat decrepit when Master Geoffrey had given it to him. He peered at it. He didn't need to read it... he knew it all by heart, really.

He took up a piece of charcoal and began to write. Then his eyes were distracted by a piece of parchment, folded and sealed with wax, which had been slipped into his old book. It was not his. He had not put it there.

He listened to the gentle and rhythmic breathing of his old master in the other part of the room and took up the parchment. There in Geoffrey's hand, was his name.

Why would Geoffrey be sending him a missive when he could speak to him at any time? They lived in the same house, shared the same space.

Puzzled, Bennet drew his nail under the fastening, a simple blob of yellow beeswax and straightened out the letter, for a letter it turned out to be.

'This will come as a surprise to you, dear Bennet.' Well he was right there.

'My dear Bennet. You are the best, the very best of men and the most able student I have ever taught and I grieve to say what I must say and at the same time rejoice that it is to you, that I entrust my whole enterprise, built up over forty years.'

What does he mean? Sad and happy at the same time?

Bennet looked once more at the superscription. Yes, the letter *was* for him. There was no error.

'I have been an astrologer for over forty years. I have not restricted myself to the great and the good, for as far as I am concerned, the little people are as much in need of our help as the great. I might have made a huge amount of money had I confined my work to the doings of those who could afford to pay great amounts for my knowledge. But I did not. And I know that you will be as am I, drawn to those little folk, for forgive me, Bennet I have cast your natal horoscope and I know you intimately from its findings.'

"Well, I have cast my own but I suppose it's not like you doing it..." said Bennet out loud.

'I have taken the liberty of forecasting for you, the whole next few months of your life.'

"What?"

'And when I am no longer here, I hope it will prove useful to you.'

"When you are no longer here?"

'For, dear boy, the pattern, the weaving of my life is drawing to an end. It is almost on its last stitches. There is little more for me to do.'

"NO!"

"I can hear you asking... 'How does he know this?' Of course I know it, for I have plotted the course of my life and I know to the last moment when I shall leave this earth."

Bennet threw down the parchment and rushed to the other room where they slept; just a cubicle really with a cloth over the doorway. Geoffrey was lying on his back sleeping, breathing gently.

Bennet went back to the parchment.

'I will leave you this year 1207, upon the fourteenth day of July at about vespers. My heart will give out and I will be no more. My testament is in the strong box and you will find that I have left everything to you.'

"Jesus!" said Bennet out loud.

'If I wake later, then I must see a priest but I do not want a doctor, for I know it will be futile. I would not bother the good man.'

A lump rose in Bennet's throat.

'I am shriven but it will do no harm to make confession again. I do not, however, think I will wake once more, except perhaps to say goodbye to you, dear boy.'

Once again, Bennet rushed to the curtained space. But Master Geoffrey was still deep in sleep.

'It has been a pleasure and an honour to teach you, Bennet and I know that you will carry on my good work. God bless you and keep you.

Until we meet again.

Geoffrey.'

Did Bennet believe him? Aye he did, for the man was a superlative astrologer, very rarely wrong.

He sat down hard upon a bench, stared at the missive again and burst into a fit of terrible tears.

*****

Master Geoffrey did not wake that day. Nor the next. Bennet hovered at the end of the bed and worried that his master had not eaten or drunk anything, nor indeed had voided his bladder or bowel. He brought up his calculations to the little room above the shop and worked diligently there, watching and waiting.

The chart for Mistress Partridge was done. Another one for the conception of a child had been completed. Bennet now began the chart for Mistress Basketwright. He found it quite challenging but at last it was done and he put down his pen.

He slept on a pallet on the floor close by his master so that he would not disturb him and he slept when he was tired, waking at odd times in the day and night and working when he could. He kept the outer door to the business closed. No new commissions were taken in.

Then on July the fourteenth just as the bell was ringing for vespers at the town's churches of St. Peter and St. Mary and the chapel of the priory close by, his master opened his eyes.

"Bennet... come close."

"Master, please...let me fetch Doctor Johannes."

"No, no. I do not wish it. Give me your hand."

Bennet took his master's hand in his own. It was cold and bony.

"I shall be gone in a moment. Listen carefully. Under the clothes in my cist there is a book. It has your signs upon it. When I am gone, take it out. But you must not read it. No. If you read it, then those things I have written there will never come to pass and I cannot help you on in your life."

His dry tongue flickered out over his lips. "You read a page a day... do you hear me. A page. No more, no less. You will need all your wits to live as you would wish to live. This book will help you. For it will tell you that you have made the right decisions. But you must swear that you will do as I ask. A page only."

Bennet, tears forming in his eyes, nodded his head " A page master... a page only per day. I swear."

"I will be watching over you. You will be a great man. I know it. I have cast your chart...remember?"

"But..."

"Now let me go. Farewell. It has been the best thing I did, taking you as apprentice. Your documents are in my cist with the paper confirming you as a master. Take it to Nicholas Barbflet the town reeve and he will register it for you and make a copy. Then none can say that you have not achieved your goal."

Geoffrey closed his eyes.

The bells ceased to toll for vespers. The house was in silence.

Bennet leaned and kissed his master on the cheek and when he rose from that action, he knew that Geoffrey Celest's spirit had gone to God.

CHAPTER TWO ~ THE BODY

B ennet wiped his eyes and, taking the key from Geoffrey's belt, went to the chest in which his master kept his private and valuable possessions.

Lifting the lid, a pang took hold of his heart. Clothes. The clothes which his master used to wear, were folded neatly into a pile. The smell of his master wafted up to him. Bennet dug in his hands and his fingers closed around a book. Was this the one which Geoffrey had indicated or was it some other?

The only way to find out was to pull it out and examine it.

Slowly, very slowly, Bennet lifted the book free.

It was bound with black leather and was about six inches in height. 'Unremarkable,' thought Bennet. However, it was the weight of the book which surprised him for it was thick with pages. His fingers longed to thumb through, as one would, a new book, never before seen. But he had promised his beloved master and he would not go back on his oath. On the cover was a symbol; that of Virgo; Astrea, the daughter of the Titans. By its side lay the symbol for Leo - the lion, Bennet's rising sign. That sign which was rising on the horizon when he came into the world and this was followed by a moon sign of Virgo; in which part of the sky the moon had been when he was born. By these symbols Bennet knew this book was his.

He set it down and looked at the body of his master rapidly cooling on its mattress. 'I must go and report the death to the priest of St. Mary's and to Master Barbflet, as my master bade me,' he said to himself.

He scrabbled further into the pile of clothes in the chest and found a parchment which looked as if it was the last will and testament of Master Celest. He scrutinised it for a few moments. This *was* the will. Where were his indentures and the letter which his master had written to confirm that he had completed his training? At the very bottom, Bennet found the document and closed the lid on all the clothes. They were his now. He smiled. His master had dressed well, even a little gaudily. His eyes strayed to the body once more. Geoffrey wore a red supertunic with a blue cotte under and a little green felted hat with red braid sat on the bed beside him. Bennet smiled again. *He* was not such a colourful man. *He* would wear the clothes with care and restraint.

Locking up the house, he walked the short distance to the town reeve's dwelling to report his master's death and then once that duty was done, he struggled up the slight hill and into the alleyway which led to the church. Would Father Torold be there at this time? He surely would, for it was barely past vespers.

The church was emptying. The small space before the south door was surging with people. Bennet was crushed against the wall.

"Excuse me. Make way there." He was moving against the flow. Best he wait for a short while. He flattened himself against the wall and watched as people shuffled out. Suddenly he felt a hand on his arm; he turned rapidly but he could not see who it was. In a flash, someone else had grasped him by the belt and pushed him hard against the wall upon which he leaned.

He felt them fumbling for the purse at his belt in order to cut the leather strap.

He pulled away and twisted and grabbing his purse with his right hand he launched himself from the wall. Whoever was trying to rob him fell back and Bennet staggered into the now almost empty porch by the door.

There were hardly any coins in his purse but he had no wish to lose them even so. Quickly, he pushed past the few loitering churchgoers in the doorway and into the darkness of the building.

It took him but a moment to find Father Torold and tell him the sad news.

"I will come immediately, young Bennet," said the priest, "Your master was a good friend to this church and of great benefit to this town. He and I had many interesting discussions about free will and the influence of the stars upon the actions of man."

"He used to come home and tell me about your theorising, father. I know that you didn't always see eye to eye about things but..."

"Ah no. We used to debate the use of astrology in choosing the timing of actions. I must say that I felt it was wholly false, and I rejected the determination of human action by the stars, on the grounds of free will."

Bennet smiled. "I doubt that argument will ever be won...by either the priest or the astrologer."

Torold took on a resigned expression. "Perhaps you and I may carry on where Master Celest and I left off."

"Meanwhile, Father Torold, please may you come and make my master fit to meet his maker? I am concerned for his soul."

"He was shriven at..."

"I know but such a sudden death..." Bennet did not like to make it known that Geoffrey had foreseen his own demise. "I would be sure that his soul passes easily and without hindrance from this world to the next."

Father Torold placed his hand upon Bennet's shoulder. "I will allow no wicked demons to drag him down to Hell, Bennet. I promise."

Bennet was about to turn away... "Or should I say *Master* Bennet now?"

Bennet nodded and smiled.

"Your master's death was unexpected and sudden. I think the

coroner should know about it."

Bennet hovered in the porch, wondering if he should explain to this priest that Master Celest had foreseen his own death almost to the very moment.

"Thank you, sir."

He was at the end of the path when Torold shouted. 'Will you take his name now he's gone."

"It is traditional. I will."

"Then, Master Celest, I will be with you shortly."

*****

Bennet let himself into the house again and stared once more at the little book he had left on the table.

Sun in Virgo, moon in Virgo, Leo rising. In short it was all that made up Bennet of Marlborough. Now Bennet *Celest* of Marlborough. Should he read the will? Ah no, perhaps not alone. He needed witnesses to verify that the business and the house were to come to him. On the following day he would seek out Master Questier, the lawyer and ask him to read it to him.

The little black book called to him. He ignored it. He made himself something to eat and once the priest had been, he ate it with no real sense of relish, even though it was all he'd eaten that day.

They would fetch his master as darkness fell and Geoffrey would be housed in the church until his interment.

He sat and waited and while he waited he stared at the book.

Why had his master forbidden him to look at more than one page a day? Why could he not look at just one page now?

He was roused from his reverie by a voice calling him from the street outside.

It was the men come to fetch the body. Bennet lit a candle and carefully trod the narrow stairs to open the outer door.

"We've come fer yer body," said the first man.

"Upstairs," said Bennet.

"Ah... that's goin'a be a bit difficult," said the second man.

"Why?"

"How'ee goin'a get the body down the stairs. No room to manooover... is there?"

The first man indicated a plank. "This 'ere thing don't bend in the middle ... see."

"I will carry him down and then you can lay him on your wood and take him out of the door."

"Nah... we'll take 'im through the winder."

"The window? Upstairs?" Bennet had grave misgivings. "What if you drop him."

"Oh, it ain't a far drop and he's dead already. Can't 'urt 'im can it?"

"No. I *will* carry him."

Bennet ran back up the steps and by the light of the candle set by the head of the stair; he picked up his master, who was not a big or heavy man. However he had not counted on the wooden state of the corpse. Rigor had set in and the body could not be moved easily.

The two men had obviously got fed up with waiting and were coming up the stairs.

"Ah. Now you see the problem," said the first man. "He's as stiff as a starched sheet."

"Window it is then, Gerald," said his mate, pulling back the shutters.

"No, no," said Bennet angrily. "That is too undignified for such a man."

The second man was pausing on the stairwell. "Either he comes out tonight by the winder or he stays here till he's less stiff."

Bennet was distraught.

"I will catch his shoulder and you his feet and we *will* get him down the stairs."

The two men sighed and resigned themselves to a tussle with the body.

Bennet gently eased his master's head around the first turn. Then he must almost stand the body up straight for the next two steps. The second man, muttering and chunnering, had to squeeze past and ease the feet through the space in the front room. There was a crack, as Master Celest's head hit the top of the wall of the stairwell. Bennet winced.

"Ah well," said the first man, sitting on the bottom step, his hands guiding the body through the door hole, "It won't 'urt 'im, will it."

Suddenly they were out in the main room and the plank of wood was once more retrieved. Master Geoffrey Celest was laid upon it and a sheet was thrown over him.

Now for the outer door.

Bennet pulled the plank of the door back as far as he could. The body would not go through easily.

With a great tug, the senior man, muttering expletives under his breath, got the first part out into the street. No one was about. Bennet was happy about that. The second man however was not paying attention and Master Celest slid from the plank to land with a thud in the mud of the road.

"Quick, get the plank out," shouted Bennet in complete desperation.

The plank came out on its edge.

They managed to get Master Geoffrey back onto it again and covered him once more.

The senior man cleared his throat. "Aye well. The winder would'a bin a better bet."

He hovered on his foot and looked pointedly to Bennet's purse.

"I should give you nothing, for you are a useless pair but…" Bennet took out some money. "Get him to the church in one piece. And make sure you pay the women for a laying out. I will know if you don't."

The two touched their forelocks in mock obeisance and marched off with their burden.

Bennet returned to the upper room and silence. And, for the first time in his life, to loneliness.

The black book seemed to take up almost the whole of his vision.

He picked it up and opened it.

Upon the first page were very few words.

'Upon the day of my death which is the first day of your life as a master astrologer - You will suffer an attempt to relieve you of your purse but it will fail.'

Bennet gasped.

"You will have difficulty getting my body from this upper room. The window is the obvious choice but the stairs will be chosen and you will drop my corpse. For which I do forgive you."

"Oh master I am so sorry," said Bennet sadly and shut the book with a snap.

*****

The temptation to read another page was overwhelming but Bennet did not give in. He slept early in the night and then rose the next day before the dawn had touched the sky with its rosy glow.

I must take this chart to Mistress Basketwright as was promised. Cottage behind the Grange barn, she'd said.

Bennet rolled up the chart and tucked it into the breast of his cotte. He locked the chest where the money was kept, bolted the shutters and doubly locked the door to the house before striding out down the marketplace. He took the Manton Road which skirted the southern moat of the castle and walked by the river for some while, deep in thought.

He must get himself a servant. He could not trust leaving the house unoccupied. Master Celest had always been at home or had left Bennet there if there was a journey to be accomplished. Quite apart from the money in the chest, there was all the expensive astrological equipment and books. Yes, he must get himself a servant and he had not the first idea how to go about it.

He thought back to his youth. His father had been a parchment maker in the town, his mother a sempstress. When he was six, his mother having died and, not being able to cope, his father had gone into the priory as a lay servant with a view to taking holy orders. Bennet went with him and this was where he learned to read and write for some of the other lay servants there were literate and were only too happy to pass on their knowledge to an inquisitive and able boy, in their spare time.

Then came the day when his father took ill and died and just before he did, he apprenticed the young Bennet to Master Celest. Bennet had been uncertain then, of his future. This eccentric man had frightened him. Thinking back, how could he have been frightened? Geoffrey had been the most patient of men, the most generous of masters and the kindest of teachers. Bennet had been twelve.

He needed to find himself a young man like he had been. Maybe an orphan, if he could find one intelligent enough.

Ah no. He wasn't thinking of taking on an *apprentice*...just a servant. But he couldn't imagine living in close proximity with someone who hadn't got a quick brain and an inquiring mind. He needed company as much as domestic help. He put the thought from him as he turned the corner of the barn and spied the cottage.

It was a substantial building of two storeys, crux built with a good deep thatch. Around and about were several small outhouses; one was obviously used as a store for withy's and rushes for basket making.

Bennet called out and the girl with the long dark plait peered myopically around the newel post of the outer stair.

"Ah it is the astrologer's man," she said.

"Master Celest now, mistress," said Bennet proudly. "My master has died and I have taken over his business."

"Well I hope that you are as good as he said he was," said the woman who came out of the door of the cottage, "I can't be paying for second rate just because you are now the only astrologer in town." She showed no emotion at the news that Master Geoffrey was no more.

"I promise you madam that my work is just as detailed and as accomplished as was my dear master's." He knew as he said it that this was not quite the truth and he doubted if it would ever be so, for Master Geoffrey had been simply amazing in the accuracy of his predictions. But then the chart contained in the breast of Bennet's cotte was not a prediction. It was not meant to be.

"Come on in then."

Bennet fished in his breast and brought out the chart he had drawn.

"Might I stretch it out here?" he asked.

"Here use these…" said the girl. He remembered her name was Christa.

She gave him four wizened apples and he weighted the corners with them.

"Now, madam. Your birth sign is that of Aries."

"What?"

"That is the sign of the ram. The sign which governs the heavens at the time you were born. This makes you somewhat impulsive and a little hot headed."

"Oh…"

"And you see here…" 'Idiot, Bennet…she cannot read or understand these symbols.'

"That you have a rising sign in Leo which is the lion."

"Oh no…a lion. That can't be good."

"It is neither good nor bad, madam." He was sure she had no idea what a lion looked like.

Bennet noticed that the girl Christa was leaning over his chart with interest.

"Your moon was in cancer when you were born… it is…"

"Oh I don't like the sound of that."

"Madam please, do not distress yourself. It means very little to you but everything to me."

"So why have I got these pains and what can I do about it?"

"Yes, I understand that this is your main concern. Please sit down, do," he said.

"Oh... oh is it so bad that I must sit down?"

"Madam, I need to ask you a rather ...personal question."

The woman sat and folded her arms under her bosom.

"Personal?"

"About your cycle and how regular it is, how you…"

She bounced up.

"I am not going to discuss that with you! You upstart. You're barely a boy. What is that sort of thing to you?"

"Madam," said Christa suddenly. "Master Astrologer has come all this way to help you. You must answer his questions or he *cannot* help you."

"I will not! Filthy beast."

Bennet was about to roll up the chart and head for the door, when Christa said. "Well, he *is* right, isn't he? And if you won't tell him, I will."

Mistress Basketwright glared at her servant.

"She is experiencing heavy flows and much pain in the lower abdomen. She has a frequent need to go to the privy and her back aches."

"Thank you Christa," smiled Bennet. "This all concurs with what I find here. The womanly parts, governed by Scorpio, are upset."

"What does that mean?" asked Christa.

"Your sun sign is in the fourth house, madam. This means that your home is very important to you... and if your home is threatened or unhappy…"

Mistress Basketwright took in a sharp breath, "Yes?"

"Then you will be unwell. And you will be unwell in that area... in which... you… *are* unwell."

"So what must she do about it?" asked Christa, coming round to his elbow and looking up into his face with her hazel eyes.

"Seek an apothecary or a cunning woman who can give you a remedy which has been gathered at the time of Scorpio with a moon in Cancer. I know there are various herbs which can help. Drink less ale and more water…"

"Pah...what nonsense," said the woman.

"You have paid me for my advice and so my advice you shall have, madam."

Christa giggled into her hand.

"Refrain from carnal relations... for a while."

"OUT! OUT!" the woman reached for her broom.

Bennet did not wait to pick up his chart. It was paid for anyway. He scurried to the door. "And eat more oily fish if you can get it."

"OUT!"

Christa followed him out, laughing. "Oh she is a silly woman."

Bennet turned and dragged his feet on the river path by the barn.

"Why she consulted an astrologer in the first place and then didn't listen to the answer..." went on Christa.

"You would be surprised how many people are willing to pay for advice which they do not heed."

Christa threw back her head and laughed. "I *would* believe it." The red of her cotte reflected on her apple cheeks.

She looked at him closely then, and he began to be a little disconcerted. She walked by his side some paces before she said.

"You really believe in what you do, don't you?"

"If I did not, I would not do it."

"And you really like to help people, don't you?"

"I do."

"Not just part the fool from his...or her money?"

"If a consulter is not happy then I would always give them their money back."

Christa gave a wry smile. "Then you must be careful, for there will be some who will tell you to your face that they are unhappy but who will take your advice. You should not give back money will' I nil' I."

"Will your mistress be one of those?"

"Not if I have any influence."

She turned on her heel and her dark plait bounced on her back. Goodbye Master Astrologer."

He was about to call out a goodbye when from the greenery by his head a wren came screeching along the hedgerow to sit in the depths of the bushes, shrieking it's alarm call. Tic, tic, tic.

"Apologies Master Wren," said Bennet, looking back once. But the girl was nowhere to be seen.

*****

Bennet was busy with calculations for the rest of the day, for some of the more wealthy inhabitants of the town requested help at almost every season, with business decisions, marital matters and work issues.

Evening came and his hand hovered over his black book.

His master's voice came into his ear as he read, 'Take care Bennet, how you deal with Mistress Basketwright. Her husband is abusive and will not tolerate interference. You will find that he mistreats her. Be careful in your dealings with her. Today you have met an influential person and they will be happy for your help. The colour red is lucky for you today. The wren will be your guide, as she will always.'

It was a few hours later when he saw the girl Christa again.

Next morning, he opened the front door on the girl who was huddled on the doorstep.

"Christa?" Her knees drawn up to her chin, she had pushed herself into the small recess by the door.

She lifted a pale and tear stained face to his.

"My mistress is dead," she said with pain in her voice. "That brute of a husband has killed her!"

CHAPTER THREE ~ THE GIRL

Once inside Christa gave way to proper tears.

"She was a silly woman but she didn't deserve that pig of a husband. She did her best, always did her best but it was never good enough."

"You say he has *killed* her?" said Bennet in horror.

"Yes. You didn't see that coming in your chart, did you, Master Astrologer?"

"Well, no...but that was because I was concentrating on her health..."

"Well if death isn't the result of poor health, then I don't know what is," said Christa with spite in her voice.

"That's not fair," said Bennet, "I wasn't looking for anything like her being *killed*."

He recalled the words of his master written in the little black book.

'But my master knew something though,' he said to himself.

"Were you there when she was...you know...when he...?"

"I was in the other room and I saw him strike her and then I saw, through the crack in the door, the mistress fall, hit her head on the hearth and lie still..."

"You didn't rush out and..."

"No, I daren't, otherwise I too would be lying dead on that floor."

"He is a violent man?"

"He's noted for it."

"What did he do next?"

"Just stormed out."

"Did he know you were there?"

"No...he thought I was in the weaving shed."

Bennet thought the situation through in his head. "He didn't see you. He doesn't know that you saw him?"

"No. When he'd gone, I made sure that she was truly dead and then I ran."

"Jesu, Christa, he'll know that you saw him *because* you ran..."

"What else was I to do?" she started to whimper again. "I wanted to get to the town reeve to tell him what I'd seen."

"You need to report it to the coroner's office at the castle... or the sheriff's office."

"I am frightened, Master Celest. What if he comes after me?"

"No one knows where you are... Do they?"

"No."

"And no one saw you...?"

"No, not really."

"Then stay here and I will go to the town reeve and ask his advice."
The girl shivered.

"How long have you been sitting outside the door?" he asked.

"Since before dawn."

"And you didn't stay at your house last night?" He wrapped a spare blanket around her shoulders.

"No...I didn't *dare* stay."

"So where *did* you go?"

"I crawled through a broken plank at the Grange barn and hid in the straw. All night. I was here on your doorstep at dawn."

"You should have told me you were here. I would have let you in."

"It is all like a bad dream, Like it never happened."

"But you are sure it did?"

"Oh yes… it happened," she said.

*****

Bennet reported the death to the town reeve who went, with a party of men, out to the cottage to question the man Basketwright and to discover the body.

The man was in his weaving shed, calmly building up the sides of a large basket. He peered at them through the forest of upright withies.

"Wife? She's gone to Chippenham to see her mother."

"When do you expect her back?"

"Well, I can't rightly say. Her mother is right poorly, you see, so it might be some time."

"We have reason to believe that she has been killed."

"Killed? Don't be daft, man. Who would want to kill my wife?"

"You?" said the town reeve.

"Nah…I wouldn't kill 'er."

"We have a report…" began Nicholas Barbflet.

"Well you can come into the 'ouse and see if you can find a body but I'm telling yer, she's in Chippenham as right as rain."

They found no body, no blood, nothing at all to indicate that Margaret Basketwright was dead.

"I told you there was nothing to see," said the basket maker. "And if you see that two faced bitch of a servant of ours, tell her she i'n't welcome 'ere any longer."

Master Barbflet, hadn't told the basket maker that it had been the servant who had seen the killing. He didn't mention her at all.

"If you have any concerns, if your wife doesn't return or get in touch within a month then let us know."

"It might be more 'an a month."

"However long it takes," said Master Barbflet with a nasty grin. Turning to walk down the path, he spoke from the side of his mouth. "We need to watch this bastard, Greaves."

"You don't believe him, sir? He's noted for *being* a bastard, if you'll allow me to say."

"Not a jot. It's too...perfect."

"Too coincidental?"

"Too... convenient."

"What do you want us to do?"

"I don't have the free number of men to put a watch on him." He gnawed his lip, "but I have a lad I can ask...one who has the right to be close by on the river."

"Fisher's lad?"

"He's a good watcher."

Perkin Fisher was the young son of the man who fished the River Kennet for the townsfolk's suppers on fish days; every Friday, Lent and other Holy days. He could keep an eye on the cottage easily.

Basketwright watched the town reeve's party walk back up the riverside path and after a while, he put down his tools and idled to the back of the weaving shed.

There, under a pile of withies was a large, lidded, circular basket, half the height of a man, and made of plaited rushes.

Basketwright lifted the lid and stared out through the door of his shed.

"Alright in there Margaret, my love, are we?" he said, nastily. A quick look in the basket would have revealed the body of his wife; a huge bloody wound to the back of her skull and her eyes staring in her head.

*****

"They found nothing," said Bennet to Christa a little while later.

"She's there...she is. Unless he's already buried her somewhere."

"Apparently he told the town reeve that she's gone to Chippenham to visit her mother," said Bennet.

"Her mother *does* live in Chippenham that's true but...she wasn't planning on visiting her as far as I know. It's a long way and she'd have to organise to go with a cart from town. I know she didn't do that."

"Tell me again what happened."

Christa sat down on a bench. Now that the shock of the moment had passed, she was quite calm.

"They were arguing."

"What about?"

"Her visit to the astrologer."

"To us... Oh Lord!"

"He had forbidden her, you see, to spend the money."

"I see..."

"But he found the chart and she told him that she'd gone to find out why it was she was unable to conceive a child. She thought it would help."

"Well she would be barren, with all that was going on in her womb."

"And Lord, don't I know; the poor woman had to put up with his thrusting and pushing every other day when the fancy took him, in order for her to get pregnant!" said Christa.

"That won't have helped her condition either," said Bennet.

"Oh...poor mistress," said Christa with a sob, "She was doing her best."

He put a consoling hand on her shoulder.

"Then when she said that you had said that she had got a problem with her womb and that she needed to see a doctor, well he saw red..."

"Saw more money being spent more like."

"He told her it was all her fault and she was useless. And he hit her hard and she fell, smashing her head."

"Well she is in a finer place now," said Bennet trying to make her feel better.

"No she isn't!" Christa sprung up crying. "She's unshriven, unmourned and dumped in an unconsecrated grave."

"Well, what can *we* do about it?"

"Find her body!"

"And how can we do that?"

"When Basketwright next takes his wares to market, that'll be Wednesday, we can go and poke around."

"He will have buried her somewhere by then. If she isn't already buried."

"There might be something there to give us a clue," said Christa in desperation.

"No... no..." Bennet backed away. "I am not going to trespass in someone's home."

"He never leaves the door locked. We could be in and out..."

"NO!"

Christa sat down and pouted.

Bennet walked to and fro. "There might be a way to unmask him."

He turned over a few of his parchments and looked for a piece of charcoal.

"My master was the best astrologer ever. He was able to tell from the positions of the stars and planets exactly what was happening in someone's life almost down to the last hour." Bennet reached for an almanac.

"He has done it for me and I must say that so far, he has been amazingly correct...about what's happening in my life now."

"How will that help us?"

"If I can do something of the same for Mistress Basketwright's life, it might tell us where her body is at the moment."

"Do you think you are as good as your master?" said Christa with a sneer.

"No, but I can try to copy how he worked."

He hunched over his parchment. "But I will need absolute quiet and no interference."

Christa sat back and gazed at the ceiling.

"Then I will busy myself. This place needs a good clean. You can tell there has been no woman in your lives for a long time." She jumped up to a beam and caught an old and dusty spider's web in her hand. Coughing, she shook it out of the window. "Where do you keep your mops and brushes?"

*****

Bennet worked all day, pausing only to go to the privy, and eat a hunk of bread with the ale he had bought from Mistress Brewster.

Christa brushed, mopped, shook blankets and dusted around him and there were several altercations between them as she came too close to his work or her actions made him sneeze.

Finally as the afternoon was drawing into evening and Christa was dozing full length on the bench by the window, Bennet laid down his pen and drew his hands across his face, rubbing his tired eyes.

"I am not the astrologer my master was. But I have done my best."

Christa jumped up. "You are not as old as your master was, you have not his experience. I am sure that, once you are established you will get better and better and will surpass him."

How very kind, thought Bennet but he said nothing.

"So what have you found out?" Christa approached him slowly.

"Mars is very important at about the time that Mistress Margaret was born. And again when she died...if she is dead..."

"She *is* dead...why won't you believe me?" said Christa angrily.

Bennet consulted his parchments and shuffled them around... "Yes...I think she is. It seems to me that the heavens have stopped revolving above her."

"So, where is she?"

"There are many elements governed by the various planets."

"Elements? What is an element?"

"Well, things like fire, or water..."

"What has that got to do with Margaret?"

Mars is a planet of action. It rules the head. Fire is Mars' element and can be helpful but it can also be violent and unpredictable like Mars. The stone associated with it is the aquamarine."

"What on earth is that?"

"It is a pale blue stone used in jewellery. It looks like water."

"Oh come on, Master Celest. You aren't making sense."

"Sorry...sorry... *I* can see the connections with things but...Oh why isn't my master here? He would see it in a flash."

"Mars is an old god...is that right?"

"Yes...an angry one."

"And so that might be Basketwright. He was certainly angry."

"And a stone was the cause of her death. But not an aquamarine."

"No... it was a large lump of flint."

"Flint... yes... that is a type of quartz."

"Oh Master Celest... Please..."

"Quartz is a healer. It brings to an end all suffering. Don't you see? It is known as the master healer and amplifies energy."

"Well it certainly didn't heal Mistress Margaret."

"It brought an end to her suffering," said Bennet. "Yes... Yes... I am on the right pathway." He began to scribble again upon his parchments.

"The natural elements surrounding her death are stone and water, particularly water with willow trees."

"Well of course they are. Master Basketwright is a maker of baskets, he uses willow to...Oh! I see."

"And rushes. They are ever present in her life...these things...and in her death." Bennet looked up.

"He has her in a basket." he said proudly."

"Oh Master Celest that was wonderful," said Christa, throwing her arms around his neck and stepping back immediately, embarrassed. "We really must go and look in some of the man's baskets."

"We really mustn't go there. He has killed once."

"Then what?"

"I will inform the town reeve that I think the body is in a basket but...I'm not certain that it will still be there by the time the reeve's men get there."

"Then you must do another calculation... did you call it. To find out if she will still be there when the men arrive."

He did not need to do that, for no sooner was the tale told to Nicholas Barbflet, upon the next moment, the young man Perkin Fisher came running into the office in the town mill.

"Sir... Sir...the man you set me to watch, he has just set a load of baskets upon his cart and he is heading down the river by the Manton path."

"It's not market day, yet," said Bennet. He turned to the young fisherman.

"Does he have a large basket on his cart? Large enough to contain a body?"

Perkin waved his hands about with excitement. "Aye he does. A big round one."

Bennet turned to Master Barbflet. "Surrounded by the element water and contained in a natural substance like willow or rush. He is planning on tipping her in the river in the fading light when there is no one to see."

It was a matter of moments to collect a few folk together, like a hue and cry, and together they all made for the cottage behind the Grange barn. It was indeed going dark now and they had to pick their way carefully along the ground.

There was Basketwright's cart loaded with his wares. There on the cart was a large round basket but there was no sign of the master basketmaker.

Greaves jumped up on the cart and steeling himself for what he might find inside, he lifted the lid. "Nothing, sir."

"Then she is already in the river," said Bennet. "Tomorrow we shall find her downstream and tangled in the rushes."

Master Barbflet swore. "Where *is* the devil?"

Bennet scanned the greying landscape. "I have no doubt that he is here somewhere. Maybe watching."

"If he has any sense, he'll flee into the forest," said Greaves.

"Leave a man at the cottage overnight...if he returns we'll know," said the town reeve.

*****

The next morning the body of Mistress Basketwright was found at the Castle Mill. It had, as Bennet had predicted, become tangled up at the edge of the river in the reeds.

"You are really good at this, aren't you?" said Christa as she emerged from the little cubicle where she had stayed the night. "You said it would…"

"The planets do not lie."

Christa sat down and began to re-plait her hair. "Oh poor Mistress Margaret. I hope they catch him and hang him slowly."

"They haven't found him yet. They've been out looking since dawn but he never went back to the cart or the house."

"Can you not do a chart or something and tell the reeve where the man is hiding?"

"Christa, I have work to do. Whilst I am looking for bodies and trying to locate felons, I am not making any money doing my job."

She carried on plaiting and then he realised that she was crying quietly. He looked down on her.

"What's the matter?"

"Nothing…it's just…I have nowhere to go."

Bennet looked around the room. Thanks to Christa's hard work of the previous day, the place was clean and tidy.

"I…don't suppose…I can't pay much of course and there would be food and lodging thrown in…but I am in need of a servant."

"A servant?"

"I don't have the time, as a *master* astrologer to do the menial tasks any longer. I used to do those jobs when my master was alive but now…"

"Now *you* need a servant?"

"There would be a private space for you there," and he pointed to the little cubby-hole at the other end of the room, "and the privy as you know is out in the yard and I would not bother you. You might do the marketing and cleaning and show in clients…"

Again Christa's arms came around his neck,

"Oh that would be wonderful." Then she drew back from him. "I will stay if you will do one thing for me."

"What's that?"

"Teach me what you know about the planets."

Bennet had not quite taken in what she had said.

"Eh?"

"I want to be able to do what you do," she said.

Bennet sighed. "Christa. In order to know how to do what I do, you must be able to read and write and add up numbers. Complex numbers. You haven't the first idea…"

"Oh yes I have."

"Oh don't be foolish. Anyway you are a girl and girls cannot be astrologers."

"I don't want to be an astrologer, I just want to learn."

"You can't. It needs a certain…"

Again, Christa pouted and flounced away. She picked up one of Bennet's parchments, flattened it on the table and peered at it.

"Well, I can't tell what *that* is…" *That* was the symbol for Sagittarius, "But this says, 'on the fourth day, at the third hour the sun will…'"

"You *can* read it?"

"My father was a priest."

"Oh!"

"Yes… he taught me to read and to do some numbers but I am sure I could learn really quickly and then I could help you."

Bennet sat down. "I don't have the time to teach."

"I would watch and learn. I am very quick to pick things up."

Under his breath, Bennet said, "I am sure you are."

"Oh please…can we just try it for a while. I promise, if I am getting in the way, I will stop doing it."

"Getting in the way?"

"Stop learning."

"I do not know you well, mistress," said Bennet, "but, what I *do* know of you on our short acquaintance is that you will probably never stop thinking."

"Do we have a bargain?"

Bennet sighed. I will regret this, he thought. And then his mind went back to the little black book which his master had left him.

The colour red was to be important. Christa wore a red dress. And did not his master tell him that he had met a person lately who would be influential in his life?

"Yes, we have a bargain," and they spat and shook hands.

"If I am to have you here in my home, then I must know a little more about you."

"What do you want to know?"

"What is your proper name...where do you come from...? How old are you?"

Christa patted down her black hair.

"Well, I am nineteen... I know that, and I come from a little village this side of Devizes. It is called All Cannings and my father was the priest there until he died... and..."

"Priest... so you are the daughter of an incumbent priest? In charge of a benefice?"

"Yes indeed... my mother died two years after I was born and my father, who was a married priest, brought me up alone."

"That must have been difficult."

Christa smiled. "That is why I am called Christa..."

"Ah yes. Do you have another name?"

"I do."

"Then..."

"My name is Christa Wren."

Bennet suddenly felt odd. "The wren will be your guide," said the voice of his old master in his ear.

CHAPTER FOUR ~ THE STINGING BEAST AND THE TWINS

B ennet had forgotten all about his little book. And so the next morning he fingered through the few pages he'd already read, to get to the next revelation.

'You will begin a search. A search which will last the rest of the year. The wren will help you. You will solve a problem but be careful of your movements over the next few days. You will acquire a servant.'

"Well, at least that is what was *meant* to happen," said Bennet to himself.

"What?" said Christa coming into the room.

"Nothing...it's nothing."

Bennet stuffed the book back under his mattress. He had moved his bed into the large upper room to allow Christa privacy in the smaller one.

Bennet looked out through the window. Two white doves from Mistress Wainwright's dovecote went wheeling across the sky, making a soft wheep, wheep sound with their wings. He noticed how dull were the colours most working people wore on the street.

"I think we must get you some different clothes," said Bennet looking back at Christa's red kirtle. "You are too recognisable in those clothes."

"You don't think that Master Basketwright will come into town to look for me?"

"I believe if he guesses that you have reported him to the authorities, then there is that distinct possibility. He is a vindictive man."

"But he would be recognised!"

"If *you* can change your appearance, then so might he."

"Oh..." said Christa with a worried expression. "What must we do?"

"I think we shall go to Madam Seconda. She trades in second hand clothes. If we buy something new then we are just advertising the fact that you have just acquired it and folk might wonder why, since you are - forgive me - only a servant."

Christa pouted. "I suppose it makes sense."

"And can we do something with your hair? It is very recognisable."

"Do what?" said Christa in alarm.

"Oh nothing... not cut it or anything, but perhaps you can wear a cap to hide it a little."

"I certainly can coming into the winter." Christa folded her hands in front of her. "I have a few things back at the house. My comb and a cap and my mother's cloak... I'd like them back."

"I forbid you to go back to that house. It's too dangerous."

"Then how *am* I to get them? They mean a lot to me. They are all I have."

Bennet tutted. "I will go. At night. Write down for me what there is and where they lie and I will fetch them... That's if the house hasn't been looted of course. Or if the basket maker has returned."

Christa reached for a pen. "You can wrap everything up in the blanket cloak and sling it over your back."

That night, shortly after vigils, Bennet crept out of the house wearing his darkest clothing. He had to be careful that he didn't meet the watch, for this was long past curfew.

He swore a few times travelling the riverside path, for the going wasn't easy but at last he reached the Grange barn. Flattening himself to the wall of the building, he peered around the corner. The door to the cottage was closed but he could see no special lock, bar or hanglock securing it. There was just the one door to the house and so he had no choice. He bent double and ran.

With one swift push and a wriggling movement, he entered the pitch black cottage.

Christa had written him a list of everything that she owned and where she had them stored. He had a good memory, honed through years of committing to mind the meanings of patterns of planets. He had no need of keeping the list but he had it in his cotte breast all the same.

First, the cloak. He scrabbled in the bottom of a chest. Finding it, he laid it out and began the search for all the other objects. He tipped them all into the middle of the blanket like cloak and tied it corner to corner.

He listened. A nightjar made its purring call - he was not afraid of that. He stepped towards the door which he had left a little open. Then he jumped out of his skin as two cats began yowling at each other in the yard very close to the property.

"Shoo... Psst! Go away!" he said in the quietest voice that they could hear and he could manage without making too much noise. They spun off into the bushes.

He craned his neck to see if any of the other cottages of the village had suddenly lit a lamp. He could see no light. No door opened. No voice challenged. The other houses were too far away.

He stepped out and quietly closed the door, throwing the wrapped bundle over his right shoulder.

Turning to run back into the complete darkness of the barn wall he came up against a tall shadow.

"Who have we here then?" said a voice.

Bennet tried to run but he simply collided with a tall figure and bounced from the rock hard muscles of the man's body.

"Stealing are we?"

"No... No. I am merely recovering... Harry?"

"Bennet?"

A hard hand came out and took his shoulder. "Quick!" They moved into the shadow of the wall.

"What are you doing here, Harry?" said Bennet.

"I need to ask you the same question, Master Astrologer!"

"Well, I am recovering some items belonging to Christa Wren - the servant girl who used to live here." Bennet fished in his cotte and came out with the list. "See here." He knew that his friend could read but it was too dark to do so.

"Ah...I wondered where she'd gone."

"What do you mean?"

"I wondered if we would have to look for another body."

"Ah, no. She's with me. The town reeve is keeping it quiet."

"Right."

"And so...what are *you* doing...?"

"Master Barbflet asked me to take the watch tonight, until matins. Then another will take my place. We are watching for Basketwright returning."

"All of you volunteers? You really think he'll come back?"

"No, I don't. I think he'll move on somewhere else," said Harry.

"I was a bit concerned. It was Christa who saw the murder. That's why she's hiding with me and I've come to fetch her things. I shall take her to Madam Seconda on Figgins Lane later, to get her a new kirtle. She sticks out like a frog in a toad pool in her red kirtle."

"Then you'd better be on your way. It'll be getting light by the time you get back."

"No word about this Harry...to anyone. Christa is scared that the basket maker will come after her."

"Best you look after her then," said Harry winking at him.

*****

Christa took his hand and squeezed it as thanks when he placed the blanket on the table. She fell on her things immediately cooing over and fondling them.

'I imagine that these things are very important to a girl,' said Bennet to himself as he watched her.

She fished out a little barbette type cap and put it on, pushing the plait now wound into a crespinette, into the back of it. "Will this do, do you think?" she said.

"Well. It does hide most of your hair and that's good. Later, we will go and buy you a kirtle."

Her eyes glittered. "Oh I wonder what the woman will have in her shop?"

"She will have, I hope, a dull dress in which you will blend into the background. We can't have you standing out in blue or pink or yellow!"

"Oh. Dull will not suit me."

"Dull might keep you alive though."

He then told her that he had met his friend Harry Glazer, at the cott.

"You didn't tell him I was here?" she said with fear in her voice.

"I did tell him. He is part of the town reeve's guard and he was set to keep an eye on the place to report if the basket man came back. He is perfectly trustworthy. He is my best friend."

He could tell that Christa was not completely convinced but she sat down and was silent.

"Now, I have been up half the night and I am going to bed. When I wake we shall go out."

"What shall I do for a few hours?"

"Read this." He took out a tatty Miscellany, a book which explained how the cosmic forces were thought to influence one's life. In the pages of this book were pictures of people personifying the planets; a woman for the moon, Jupiter as a bishop, Mars as a soldier.

"See what sense you can make of it and we shall discuss it when I wake."

He lay down on the bed, turned his face to the wall and was silent.

Christa took the book to her own bed and, sitting with her back to the wall, she let it rest on her knees and thumbed through the pages.

The pictures were very colourful and the Latin easy. Soon, Christa was totally absorbed.

After a short while there came a voice from the downstairs room. "Master Astrologer, are you here?"

Christa listened, holding her breath. Surely they would not come up to the private quarters.

The voice called out again.

'Oh why has the master not locked the outer door,' said Christa to herself.

"I am coming," said Bennet sleepily, "I won't be a moment."

He saw Christa through the doorway and put his fingers to his lips and struggled up from his bed.

She heard him descend the stairs.

"Oh, Madam Seconda, it is pleasant to see you. I was planning a visit to you later. My...cousin is staying with me and she needs a new kirtle..."

"Yes, Harry Glazer told me you had a 'guest'. He suggested I come to you, so that it all might remain...secret. So you need not travel the street."

"Ah...so you know."

"I do. And let me tell you, I will say nothing at all...nothing about the young lady being here. That beast of a man Basketwright deserves to swing."

"Thank you for your concern and for your confidentiality."

"I have brought some kirtles. Of course I don't know the size of the young lady, whether she be tall or small..."

"Small," said Christa as she came down to the last step. "I am but four feet eleven."

Madam Seconda smiled. "Then this one would be perfect, I think."

Christa stared at it. It was a dull brown green. The wool was not good quality but it would do quite well for the oncoming autumn and winter.

Christa's eyes strayed over a lovely deep lavender cotte, which the woman had brought with her, but she knew that it would never do.

"I will try it."

Once the dress had been tried on and Madam Seconda had been paid, Christa searched out, from her possessions, a plain leather belt which had seen better days. It was scuffed and bald in patches but it was not as rich in colour as was the red one she wore with the red cotte and would blend in. She wound it around her waist.

"It was my mother's, my father told me. I have a fondness for it even though it is a bit scruffy."

"Scruffy is fine!" said Bennet with a chuckle. "You'll blend in perfectly."

Christa wrinkled her nose. "I look like I have fallen into a dung pile. This is a horrible colour."

"I promise you may have whatever colour you like when Master Basketwright is apprehended and you are no longer in danger."

And he went back to bed.

"I will keep you to that," said Christa to herself. Though she had no idea how she would do it.

*****

Bennet awoke with a start just before midday.

"I have slept over long."

"The ale is stale. Shall I go and fetch some more?"

"If you feel confident that you can go out into the street. You know where Mistress Brewster has her premises?"

"Up the lane by the old chandlers."

"Then take this jug," said Bennet, "and keep your head down.

He dropped a coin into her hand.

He watched her from the upper window, thread her way through the crowd of the end of the market place and disappear up the lane.

47

'She blends in perfectly,' he said to himself, very happy with what they'd been able to achieve.

Then he took hold of a piece of parchment and began some computations for a client who wanted to expand his business and needed to know if the investment would pay off.

He was so engrossed he did not hear Christa return.

She was suddenly at his shoulder. "So what do you see there?"

"Quite an event, actually."

"Oh what?" She poured the ale into two cups.

"A tempest of the sun."

"Is that good... or bad?"

"It is something that only happens every so often. And it is good and bad in degrees."

"You mean that to some it is good, to others bad."

"That is the gist of it," he said.

"So what would it mean for me?"

"For you. I don't know, for I don't know anything about you"

Well then. You had better know," said Christa cheekily. "I was born at the end of 1189 when King Richard was on the throne, though he was never here, they tell me."

"That is correct. He spent much of the time abroad."

"My father recorded my birth in his big bible and so I know when I was born. And I am nearly nineteen."

Bennet turned his gaze over his shoulder. "And when was that?"

"Upon the nones of November. And he told me it was about midday, for he had just rung the bell for the midday service. And it was a Monday!"

"And it was in All Cannings?"

"It was. Can you tell anything from that?"

Bennet chuckled "But of course I can. Just wait."

He drew a fresh piece of parchment to him and began to scribble.

Christa watched as the parchment became filled with symbols and letters, numbers and calculations.

"Your sun sign is Scorpio - the stinging beast and your moon is in Virgo - the maiden. You have a rising sign of Capricorn - the goat."

"Oooh."

"And so this action in the sun will mean that…"

"Yes?"

"You will not go anywhere for quite a while!" She hit him playfully with a piece of rolled up parchment.

"No… truly. It means that everything is stuck until the fire in the sun passes and then things will get…"

"Yes?"

"Quite hot."

"But it is approaching autumn. Things are getting cooler!"

"Hot as in…" His eye caught hers, "difficult."

"You are making this up."

"I never make anything up."

Christa's eyes grew round. "And what will it mean for you?"

Bennet looked down at his original calculation. "It will mean that it is not good for anyone considering putting money into a venture. It will not be good for my client, for example. He would be well advised to wait for a better time. Nothing will happen for a while."

"But for you?"

"For a sun sign Virgo, Leo rising, moon in Virgo…?"

"Is that you?"

He nodded. "It will be a time of contemplation, a time for thinking and weighing up."

"And then?"

"A time for action."

Again her eyes were wide. "What kind of action?"

"The seventh house…commitments and loyalties. It looks as if they will be tested."

"And then?"

"A decision will be reached which has a profound effect upon life."

"And you can tell all that, from a few scribbles on parchment."

"Of course...if you know what you're looking for."

"I wish I had the money for you to tell me everything I want to know."

Bennet laughed. "People think that is what they want. People imagine that they would be very happy knowing but actually, it's not really very good to know everything."

Christa looked deep into his eyes.

"Don't you even want to know?"

"No, not really." And that reminded him, he had not looked at his little black book yesterday. He would be a day late if he didn't do it soon.

"Off you go. There is some bacon in the small pantry out in the yard. We shall have it for dinner."

Christa sighed. "Yes sir."

"I don't need that, thank you," said Bennet, laughing. "Just call me Bennet."

When she'd gone, he brought out the little black book.

'There is much turmoil in your mind. You will try to keep your mind on your work but it will be difficult until you solve the problem that arose yesterday. You will make a bargain which you are unsure you will be able to keep.'

"Oh God! I do believe I have," said Bennet to himself.

*****

"How many planets are there in the heavens?" asked Christa when they'd eaten dinner and she and Bennet were once more in his work room.

"There are the Sun and the Moon, these are known as the luminaries, plus the five planets, Mercury, Venus, Mars, Jupiter and Saturn and all of them rotate around the earth."

"But there are lots of stars in the sky. Are they all of them the same as these planets?"

"Ah no."

"What then?"

"Planets remain fixed but stars move about... in the main..."

"And this is why you have to chase them around the heavens all the time? To look at them?"

"We plot the courses as astronomers would, yes but as astrologers we are really interested in the planets. These are the bodies which influence lives and events. The stars make up the constellations."

"Constipations?"

"Constellations."

"So what is happening at the moment?"

Bennet sighed. "At this very moment there is a transit of Mercury."

"Oooh. What does that mean?"

"The planet Mercury governs Scorpio. And that means that at this very moment there is a really annoying Scorpio sun sign passing through the room, who is asking me too many questions."

Christa looked offended.

"I shall go and get us something for our supper then."

"Please do...there is money in the pot and be careful. Speak to no one."

He heard the outer door bang and went back to his calculations.

"Transits of Mercury can only occur when the Earth is aligned with a node of Mercury's orbit," he said out loud with a chuckle, "and that will not happen until November. And when it does..."

"Master Celest!" A voice shouted from the main room. The door closed again.

"A moment please." Bennet covered his work and made for the exit. He swivelled himself to lock it.

"Oh I am glad you are in."

He turned.

There in the middle of the room in a blue kirtle, upon which was dangling a large silver pilgrim ampulla, was the most gorgeous creature he had ever seen.

"I am here to help," said Bennet with a constriction of the throat and a slight bow of the head.

"I have heard say the astrologer of Marlborough, is second to none, Master Celest."

"That is kind," he said bowing and not wishing to disabuse her of the fact that she was probably talking about his master.

"Though I must admit I had not thought to find that the well-respected astrologer was so young."

"Ah...yes..."

"But never mind."

The woman looked pointedly to a stool. Now Bennet realised that there was another woman in the room. An older woman dressed in a dark saffron kirtle with a head cloth wound around a rather ugly head and secured with large pins.

Bennet looked the young woman over as he brought her a stool.

"This is my woman, Asceline."

"Mistresses. What might I do for you?"

The beautiful young woman, for Bennet had decided that she was very beautiful, leaned forward on her stool. "I find myself, sir, in a difficult place."

Bennet drew his brows together. "Difficult?"

"I must make a decision very soon and... well, frankly, I know not what to do."

"And my mistress was advised, Master Celest, to bring her problem to you," said the woman Asceline, in a dark and deep voice.

"Right." Bennet cleared his throat and reached for a piece of parchment. "And your name is?"

He was busy writing the date at the top of the page when he heard her say.

"Matilda Ferrers."

"Right, Mistress Ferrers. What is the nature of your... difficulty."

A look passed between the two women.

"It is most vexing," said the younger woman. "But it appears that

52

in six months' time..."

"Ah no, mistress..." said Bennet standing abruptly. "I am an astrologer. I am not an apothecary. If you have a problem which requires interference..."

"Oh no..." The girl laughed, a rather forced but attractive sound. "Nothing like that. I can assure you, sir, I am still a maid. No, I would not break the law of God and the land and involve another in..."

Bennet sat back down, his face colouring a little at his mistake. "Then...?"

"In six months' time I am to be married."

"Ah..." said Bennet with a relieved sigh and nervous smile.

"But I have two suitors you see. My father has, most generously provided me with two prospective husbands and...well... I know not which to choose."

"Ah, I see. You wish me to discover which of these two young men are most suitable for you."

"Alas, neither is young. But they are both wealthy and presentable. And only one has been a widower."

"Right." He looked her over. 'If I am not much mistaken, this woman has Gemini rising Her face is quite expressive. She gives the impression of being full of energy, even when resting. She has a fair complexion and hair and has a high forehead with a long, straight nose. She sits well on her stool, is confident and... ahem... somewhat alluring. Oh yes... and as we get to know her, she will be very talkative. But I would not exactly trust everything she says,' he said to himself.

"I will need to know the date of birth of you all. I will need to know where they were born and exactly at what time," he said rather quickly, to cover the long pause.

Matilda Ferrers smiled and an exquisite pain launched itself from his heart to his diaphragm. He sat.

"My birth was accomplished in Hungerford, fifteen days into June and I came forth at the hour of Matins, about half way through the mass so they tell me in the year of the battle of Hattin in the Holy

Lands."

Bennet scribbled 1187. That was an odd way for a woman to describe a natal day.

"And the good gentlemen?"

"One, Henry, was born in 1157, upon the fifteenth day of August in Northampton at the hour of Terce. Not one moment before or after. And the other, in Normandy..."

"Ah where in Normandy?"

"Rouen."

"I see."

"Does that make a difference?"

"It does not *really*; only that it's another piece of sky... over Normandy. It is not the same as England."

"Oh... where was I? Oh yes. Gerard was born in October on the nones at an hour after darkness, in 1168"

Bennet wrote down, '27th October at the thirteenth hour of the day, 1168'

"Well... I will be able to calculate for you your sun signs, your rising signs and thus I will be able to assess the compatibility of you all."

He rose again.

"But I must warn you. If I find that neither of the two gentlemen and yourself is at all compatible, then I am bound by my astrologer's oath, to tell you so. I hope this is clear?"

"Perfectly." Mistress Ferrers rose to a stately height. "Of course my father will have the final say. I will leave the charts for him to peruse. But I have a little interest."

Bennet's eyebrows came together. "You are saying you have little interest in the man to whom you are to be tied in matrimony?"

"Very little."

"Ah... right."

"I would, as I say, just like to know, which is the better man."

"Then, madam, I can tell you that," and he bowed his head. "In three days' time."

Money changed hands and, as Bennet was storing it away, Christa returned. She opened the door onto Mistress Ferrers and the two jostled each other.

"Oh I beg your pardon," said Christa, making way for the taller woman.

Matilda Ferrers looked down her nose and as stately as a sailing ship, she floated down the road.

Christa looked after her.

"That one's got no manners!" she said.

*****

For two days Bennet was very busy. Upon the first day after the visit of Mistress Ferrers, two commissions, one about the choosing of a date for a christening and another for the signing of a lease, came in to him. These were relatively easy to complete.

He then started upon the chart of the woman Matilda and those of her suitors. He worked diligently upon the first day and thumbing through his little book at night, alone in his bed, he began to feel uncertain about his working of the chart.

'You will receive a commission which will cause you some disquiet. Listen to your heart. All astrologers must do this from time to time. It is not just a matter of mathematics and charts. There are two pathways open to you. Take that which feels right.'

Bennet read it again. "Two pathways?" Was his master referring to the two suitors of Mistress Ferrers?

He slept fitfully that night and rose with a headache and in an ill humour.

Christa and he argued that morning about what they should eat for supper and she went off to market in a huff.

Bennet sat down to 'break the back' as his old master used to say, of the work on his table.

Eyes down, the symbols swam before him. The woman who had

commissioned the chart began to reveal herself.

"Well!" said Bennet tipping his chair back on its legs. "If this lady is a virgin, then I suppose I'm the Pope!"

However, that fact, that lie in itself should not prevent him from digging deeper into her personality. Many women claimed virginity. It wasn't exactly a crime. But it was a lie and where there was one lie, there were others...perhaps. It was said in the astrological art, that negative Geminis were liars. By her chart, this woman could be a negative Gemini.

He worked on.

'She moves from one thing to another like the beautiful butterfly she is,' said Bennet to himself. 'She conceals her true nature from the world; all anyone ever sees is the lovely exterior. She does not love... she possesses. That does not bode well for a future with either man,' he told himself.

He left her chart and went on to the older man, Henry. A kind and open hearted Leo. Hmmm. Would he wish such a creature on an elderly widower with such a caring nature? She would dominate and destroy him.

Then he plotted the chart of the other man, Gerard. Here was a completely different case.

Avaricious, devious, secretive and self-centred, Gerard was quite a match for Mistress Ferrers. They would spark, fight, plot together and make up in spectacular ways. Yes, this was a good match. They could go far these two. They both had the ability to make money, but together, they could make much of it. As long as one partner did not become dominant; then there would be blood spilt.

Bennet stared at all three charts.

It had begun to rain earlier and now it was raining hard. He got up, went to the window and, reaching for the shutter to close it, noticed a man lurking under the overhanging roof of the fleshmongers directly across the road.

"Pah...do not be so oversensitive; it's probably just a man sheltering from the rain. He closed the shutter.

Yawning and stretching his back, he heard the front door bang and the locking bar go down.

"Christa?"

"Oh... Bennet... Bennet."

"Whatever is it?"

She came surging up the stairs out of breath and absolutely soaked. She tripped on the last step and the food she'd been carrying in her basket tipped over the floorboards.

"Why have you been so long? You better get out of that wet kirtle and put on your old red one. Here, give me your wet cap..."

"I've been waiting...waiting to come home into the house."

"Whatever for?"

"He's found me...he's seen me. He knows where I am."

"What do you mean?"

"Basketwright...he knows I am here!"

HUNTING THE WREN

CHAPTER FIVE ~ THE SEDUCTION

"What do you mean he knows you are here?"

"I saw him in the street."

"Basketwright?"

Christa ran into her little room and stripped off her clothes behind the curtain.

"He was standing under the fleshmonger's awning."

"Ah yes. I saw him."

"He's shaved his beard and cut his hair. But I'd know him anywhere."

"I thought he might change his looks," said Bennet. "But when I saw him, he wasn't looking at you or even at the house. He was staring down the road towards St. Peter's."

"I waited until he wasn't looking our way and slipped in quickly."

She came out wrapped in her blanket. Her unbound black hair gleamed like a crow's back in the low light.

"Then if he is in town, we must make it known to the town reeve." Bennet reached for his green cloak. "I'll go now. No time like the present."

The rain was coming down in torrents as Bennet splashed his way a few doors up to the Barbflet house. Dispensing with politeness he banged on the panel.

Master Barbflet himself opened the door.

"Master Celest... come in... quickly."

"Master Barbflet, the man...he's here." Bennet's nose dripped water. "He has been seen but he has changed his appearance."

"Basketwright?"

"You are no longer looking for a man with a brown beard and shoulder length hair. I saw him and he was wearing a brown cloak with a green brown cotte under and a hood of tawny, that dusky yellow brown favoured by men at the moment."

"Has he seen you...either of you?"

"It's hard to say. Christa was out in the town shopping when she spotted him and I saw him moments before she came in. But the rain was coming down hard. Perhaps he did not see past the sheet of water."

"Let us hope not."

Barbflet turned him round. "Take care and do not answer the door to strangers."

"Master Barbflet, most of my customers are strangers. I must of necessity."

The town reeve sighed. "I can do nothing for you at the moment. We shall scour the town and if we apprehend him, we will let you know. Meanwhile, take care. Lock and bar all your doors."

He opened his own door. "God keep you Bennet."

"And you, sir."

Bennet hunched over and ran back to the house. He put the key in the lock and called out "It's me Christa."

"I have been watching him through the crack in the shutter."

"Is he still there?" said Bennet, shaking out his cloak and hanging it on a peg to dry.

"He has moved to the end of Chandler's Yard. There is better shelter there," she said.

"Has he been watching the house?"

"No. He watches everything. Searching people."

"Well there are fewer out now in this rain. They have all run for cover."

"He watched you come from the town reeve's house but once he had seen you, he took his eyes from you."

"Good. That means he does not know who I am."

"What are we to do?"

"We do not panic. The town reeve is sending out men to catch him. We must just wait."

Christa let out a huge sigh. "I feel so much safer with you around." She started to towel her hair dry.

"Look. Here is my longstaff. It will do some damage to man should you catch him on the head. It will allow you to escape if I am not here. I would offer you my bow but I do not think you could draw it."

He nodded to the corner of the room where lay both weapons. "Take it downstairs."

"Can *you* use these?"

"I'll have you know, that my friend Harry and I have been the champions in this town with the bow," he smiled proudly.

"Oh…"

"And I am handy with the quarterstaff, I promise you."

"Then I do feel much safer," she said.

Christa disappeared back into the cubby hole and came out buckling on her red belt over her red cotte.

"How have you done with your charts whilst I have been away?" She could not restrain herself from one more peek through the crack in the shutter at the road outside and particularly Chandler's Yard. The man had gone.

The rain was still drumming on the roof and on the roadway outside.

"It's mortal dark. Light a candle and I will show you."

Bennet sorted his parchments and stood looking down at them, fingering his clean shaven chin.

"It has been a revelation."

"Oh?"

"The woman is not what she seems."

"Well...I did say, though I only got a little look at her..."

"She lies as easily as some people breathe."

"Oh no! You can tell this?"

"Sadly, yes, I can. And only one man would be her match."

"Gerard?"

"How did you know?"

"I don't know...I just did."

They both sat down at the table.

"What I do not understand is why this woman comes to me and pays me money to ask such a question when I think she already knows the answer."

"Maybe she just wishes to have it clarified. Or her father does."

Bennet crossed his arms over his breast. "Do you know what? I think she already knows this Gerard quite well."

"Will you tell her?"

"Ah no. I will tell her what she paid me to find out. Which man is the best match for her."

He pointed at Henry's chart with its circle full of crossing lines and blocks of shading.

"This is the chart of a good, kind openhearted man who would make her very happy, in that he would treat her like a daughter and, because he is able, would buy her anything her heart desires."

"Oh then he is the man for her... is he?"

"Ah no. We must think not only about the person who has paid the fee but the person to whom we owe truth and moral rightness."

"You mean that it might be good for her but not for him?"

"That is precisely what I mean," said Bennet. "She would destroy him, his peace of mind."

"Whereas the other?" said Christa leaning her chin on her hands and looking up at him with her hazel eyes.

"They are a likeness. They have the same grasping nature and will do well together. Oh, they will fall out often but they will make up and move on."

"So you will tell Mistress Whatsername... Ferret...?"

Bennet laughed out loud. "Ferrers."

"That Gerard is the one for her."

"I will."

"And there will be no... hardship to the other man? This Gerard. He will not mind that she is a scheming..."

"Hussy? Not a jot!"

Christa giggled. "Then they are a good pair."

*****

That night, Bennet lay in his bed and after wishing Christa good night, behind her curtain, he scrabbled underneath him for his black book.

'You will be fooled. But you will not be fooled. Act with your head and not with your emotions. There is danger in lust and you must avoid it. If you do not, then you must fall back upon your wits.'

"Well, at least he thinks I have some wits," said Bennet snuggling down under his blankets. "Yes I do. And yes...I can use them."

The next morning was dry and mopping up in the street had begun when Bennet and Christa rose. She gave a cursory glance out of the front window just in case the man Basketwright was still observing the marketplace, but no, he was not there.

"Do we keep the door closed?" she asked. "It's not what you'd normally do is it?"

Bennet pulled his grey, or rather his old master's grey cotte over his head. "No. I have the door open so that clients can come and go."

"That woman comes today doesn't she? Ferret?"

"Fer-rers. - Yes. It would be best if you weren't here when she does."

Christa laughed. "Oh, you think there will be some trouble?"

"Not at all. I just think it better if we are alone, for what I shall be telling her, is for her ears only."

"Oh. You *are* going to tell her that she's a horror then?"

"I will do nothing of the sort."

Christa chuckled and drew on an apron. "Then I am for the yard at the back. There is a deal of rubbish there which needs clearing."

"Ah yes. I am sorry to say that my old master was a hoarder. He would throw nothing away and so the little outhouse is full of rubbish."

"That will take me all morning," said Christa as she scuttled down the stairs.

She called up. "Take care."

Bennet sat down and scrabbled at his disorderly hair.

Now he looked at a chart for Master Metier, the town goldsmith. The question he wanted answering was should he put money into a venture with another merchant who needed capital to buy furs abroad?

The morning progressed. Two clients came in. One a merchant from the top end of town who needed to know the best time to turn his hoarded coins in order to make more of them and a young lady who wished to know the sex of her unborn child. This one Bennet did not accept for this was a matter for God alone and not for astrology. However, he did say that he would cast a horoscope for the child when it was born.

Christa came in and washed her hands.

"My goodness, what rubbish your master did collect. Broken stools, chair legs, mouldy apples, old pens... And all so dirty and dusty too. Look at me."

Bennet looked up. There were smuts on her apron and smears of dirt on her face.

He laughed at the cobwebs decorating her cap and hair.

"You look perfect to me," he said and went back to his computations.

Christa watched him for a while. And then began to make them something for dinner, which they took at the fifth hour of the day.

All cleared away, Christa went back to her sorting and cleaning in the yard.

It was about midday when Mistress Ferrers and her servant arrived in the ground floor chamber. Bennet came out of the work room and locked the door.

"Mistress." He bowed his head.

The ugly servant woman looked round for somewhere to sit.

"Master Celest, please, I would like to be alone with you when you reveal to me the results of your labours."

"Oh?"

"Might we go somewhere... private."

"I never allow anyone into my workroom, mistress, said Bennet. "I have valuable equipment there. Valuable, you understand only to an astrologer... to no one else. And there are charts for clients which must remain confidential. It is my rule."

"Then maybe we might go and sit in comfort in your room upstairs."

Bennet looked her up and down. Her golden hair was plaited around her head, leaving just a little loose under a silver filet. Her slim figure was encased in fine wool of a beautiful lavender colour.

"Then mistress, please precede me, but watch the stairs at the turn, it can defeat some with its shallowness."

Bennet followed her, a foot behind and watched as her shapely behind swayed from right to left right before his nose, as she trod.

"Please sit here. This is the most comfortable chair."

She lowered herself languidly into the seat and peered at him under her eyelashes.

'Oh my!' he said to himself, 'she is a *very* beautiful woman.'

"Now...I must just go to fetch the charts...just a moment."

He ran down the stairs and into his workroom pausing only to unlock the door and throw a glance at the maidservant who had decided to have a nap leaning against the wall.

On the way back, Bennet got a better look and noticed that the woman had quite a dark moustache. Ah well... some older swarthier skinned women did.

He scurried up the stairs again.

"Mistress Ferrers. Here are the charts drawn up for you. These belong to you and they can be taken away by you so that you might show them to your father and he might know that the work has been completed."

"That is good. Yes."

"You may, if you wish, also show them to another astrologer for a second opinion should you need one."

Matilda Ferrers came a little closer.

"Might I look at them?"

"Certainly."

Bennet stretched out the first chart, Mistress Ferrers' own. "This is you Mistress Fe..."

"Please call me Matilda."

"You have your sun in Gemini, the twins. This sign is compatible with some others of the zodiac, namely..."

The woman snuggled up to him and placed her hand on his knee, whilst she looked at the complexities of the chart.

"Ahem, namely erm... Libra the scales and Aquarius... the erm... water bearer."

Her hand had moved a little further up his leg. He closed his own around it in order to move her hand away and took a deep breath. "Other Geminis will be, of course, in tune with how you... behave; the air signs in general are compatible." He realised he was gabbling. It was getting rather hot in the room.

He moved away on his stool.

"Now we have two men who are desirous..." 'Oh my God...why did I say desirous?'" Matilda followed him and looked deep into his eyes.

"Master Celest? What is your given name."

Bennet cleared his throat. "Bennet."

"Bennet... Such a masterful name."

"It means blessed I'm told, Mistress."

"Matilda... please."

Bennet heard a noise from downstairs and was grateful for the intrusion.

"Ah that will be my servant..." He attempted to rise.

"It is my maid coming back from the privy. Nothing more," said Ferrers, taking hold of Bennet's chin and pointing it to her own.

He pulled away "One is a Leo and the other a Scorpio... one fire and one water."

"The moment I saw you, Bennet Celest, I knew that I loved you."

"Mistress please...I am trying to..."

"I knew...I wanted you."

"Now fire will douse water, as you know and your own sign is an air sign and water is made bubbly by air..."

"What is your own sign, sir?" she asked suddenly.

"I am a Virgo, mistress...the virgin..."

"Are you really, Master Bennet?" she said suggestively.

"Well...yes but..."

He took up his explanation again. "If fire is applied to water it boils..."

"And if the air of Gemini is applied to the earth of Virgo..?"

"It becomes...fertile..." said Bennet as her lips closed over his.

"Then shall we see if that is true?" she mumbled.

She pinched him playfully on the arm, took his hand and levered him up from the stool.

As she did so, she brushed his body with hers and Bennet felt a frisson pass through him. He allowed her to put her arms languidly around his neck.

"Lead me to the bed..." she whispered.

Stumbling and kissing, Mistress Ferrers trying hard to get hold of the stuff of his cotte to raise it above his head, they tumbled onto the mattress in the corner of the room.

Mistress Ferrers fell uppermost and almost in one movement managed to remove her kirtle and shift as if they were one garment. As it came over her head, her hair fell loose and the filet containing it fell to the floor with a rattle.

"Oh God..." said Bennet, as she managed to get her hand into his braies.

*****

The woman was now totally naked.

As much as Bennet was desirous of her, there was a little bell ringing an alarm in the back of his head. She leaned down and covered his lips with hers again pushing her body into his. She moaned as once more she fiddled in his braies.

"Ah No!" answered Bennet, flailing for her hand.

He heard a clomping sound coming up the stairs.

'Oh God! Who the Hell was this? Please God let it not be Christa!'

No, it wouldn't be Christa with such a heavy tread.

A dark headed man came into view at the head of the stairs.

"Oh Almighty God!" said Matilda, sitting up and clutching her discarded linen shift to her body.

"What the Hell is going on here?" said a deep voice.

"Sir...I..." said Bennet breathily, without any idea of how to finish the sentence.

"Oh God!" cried Matilda again with all ardour quenched. "It is my husband!"

"Husband...but..."

The man grabbed Matilda's wrist and yanked her up. "I suppose she told you she was unmarried."

"I was casting her charts," said Bennet, scrambling up, all desire fled. He tucked his shirt into his braies.

"Ha! Is that what they call it? A fine story! *This* can be all about town in a very few heartbeats," said the man.

Bennet's ears picked up an insistent banging.

"What have you done with my servant?"

He pushed past them and stumbled down the stairs going to the back door, his heart hammering; it had been barred from the inside.

He undid it and there on the other side of it was Christa, filthy, dishevelled and as angry as a swarm of wasps..

"Why did you lock me out? I have been yelling from Midday to Vespers."

"I didn't," said Bennet angrily.

"Well the door didn't bolt itself!"

Christa looked at him carefully. "You look like…"

He carried on trying to make himself presentable.

"What on earth...?" she said.

He rubbed his hands through his hair and said with a grittiness which was nothing like his usual tone. "Right!"

He turned and with a face as hard and sharp as an executioner's axe, he walked back into the consulting room.

The man was there but Matilda was still upstairs, trying to make herself presentable.

"Now see here… I know what a tease my wife is."

"She's no more your wife than I am."

"What?"

"I think you had both better get out now, *Mistress Asceline*." Bennet's eyes strayed to the kirtle and headdress the 'woman' had discarded on the floor and had unsuccessfully pushed behind a chest to hide.

"I am willing to forget all about this if you'll give me three shillings. I think that's a fair price. Then I won't have to tell the whole town that the astrologer attacked my poor wife and tried to rape her."

Christa came in after Bennet and stood at his elbow. "Rape her?"

"Yes, young lady. I saw it with my own eyes."

"Then your own eyes are deficient sir," said Christa, "for, I saw *you* not three days ago dressed as a woman and calling herself Mistress Asceline...How would that story be received in the town? You like to wear women's clothing do you?"

The man stood up tall. "You have defiled my wife, sir."

"I can prove that you are not her husband."

Christa turned to him with a strange look.

"I can take my chart to any other astrologer you name and he will say, as do I, that you call yourself Gerard and are nothing but a pimp. Upon my calculations...you and Matilda Ferrers or whatever your real names are, are nothing but cheap tricksters, blackmailing unsuspecting, if foolish men, of the town out of their money."

"It's a trick then?" said Christa.

"Yes. And I'll pay *nothing.*"

Matilda was now coming down the stairs. Her hair was still free but her clothes were now back on her body.

"Leave it, John."

"I won't leave it."

"Christa run down to the town reeve and..." began Bennet.

The two felons exchanged a glance.

"Leave it John," said Matilda again. Her eyes swivelled to the work room, the room where Bennet kept all the most precious equipment and his money box. The door was open. Idiot! In his haste to collect the charts and return to Matilda, he had not re-locked it. He noticed his astrolabe was perched on the table by the door. He certainly hadn't left it *there*.

"Christa, go and check the money box."

The two impersonating felons then tried quickly for the outer door but Bennet was there before them, with his quarterstaff in his hand. He tripped the man with a swipe to the ankles and pointed the end of it at the sneering woman.

'However did I think her beautiful,' he said to himself.

"Gone Bennet," said Christa. "The lock forced."

The Ferrers woman rose up to her full height and made a grab for the armillary sphere.

Bennet was there first and clutched it to his bosom..

Without being asked, Christa came forward and snatched at the recumbent man's purse which was heavy with coin.

"I suppose it's all in here?"

The man, clutching his ankle, stared up at her defiantly. "You'll have to count it - shorty!"

Without another word, Christa raised her foot and caught the man a blow in the cods which made Bennet's eyes water. The man doubled up.

"Us shorties have a way with things," said Christa nastily. "And for that we are just the right height."

"And the rest?" said Bennet.

The woman Matilda now sighed. She reached behind the small table by the door and lifted two pouches from the floor.

"In here."

"I suppose you would have taken them as you left? After your... deception?"

Matilda smiled the beautiful smile which had so captivated him.

"How did you know?" she said.

"Mistress, I am an astrologer. I know things."

"There's nothing he doesn't know," said Christa proudly, above the retching sound of the man on the floor.

The woman lifted Gerard up. He staggered. But all of a sudden he made a move towards Bennet who, in one movement, brought the armillary sphere down on his head. 'Not too hard Bennet,' he chuckled to himself, 'you don't want to break it. Your sphere that is!'

The man staggered into the Ferrers woman.

"Now get out both of you!"

"You'll say nothing...?"

"If you don't."

"But if you *do*..." Christa came up to the woman. She barely reached her bosom.

"Then one dark night you'll find those lovely blonde locks floating in the River Kennet." Christa had her little eating knife in her hand and with one swipe she cut off a small lock of Matilda's hair.

"Like that."

Matilda gasped, took hold of her partner and pushing him before her, fled the house.

Bennet and Christa were left staring into the empty door space.

"Put the money back Christa."

"Yeah…"

She was going to say nothing about this attempted seduction but upon returning to the room he was still standing there, holding his astrolabe, with a stupid, dull witted look on his face.

"Whatever did you think you were doing?"

"*I* was doing nothing."

She put her hands on her waist.

"*She* was the one who was *doing*."

"But you did know…didn't you?" she asked.

"I knew something wasn't right, as I said."

Christa reached up and took hold of him and planted a kiss on his cheek.

"You really are very good at this aren't you?

*****

CHAPTER SIX ~ ATTACK!

Bennet dreaded reading the entry in the little black book that night, for fear of censure by his dead master but it was not at all as bad as he'd feared.

'Your baser nature almost gets the better of you today. You will, however, rise above it. Money will be an issue today and you will realise that you must take greater care of that which you have.'

As he laid his head upon the pillow that night, he vowed to remove more of the money he had stored in his strong box, to the Jews on Silver Street for safekeeping and to have new locks put onto his property.

'A man will have the heavens come down on his head.'

Well that was true...certainly; Bennet giggled to himself and was glad his master's armillary sphere had come to no major harm.

Next day, leaving Christa in the house, he jogged down to Master Lockyer, the locksmith who worked on the Marsh and arranged for new and better locks to be fixed to the outer doors and to the workroom. When the man came to the house, he would discuss buying a new and more sturdy strong box.

On the way home, he passed a woman he recognised and for some reason stopped to speak.

"Mistress Alleyn, it is pleasant to see you."

"Master Astrologer, I am surprised you remember me."

"But madam, I remember you well. Tell me how is your little daughter... now... let me think... Alys, I believe?"

"Yes indeed. What a good memory you have! She is well, thank you and just the child you said she'd be two years ago when she came into the world."

"Goodness me, two years..."

They walked along, exchanging information and pleasantries until Mistress Alleyn must leave him and go across the road into the fleshmongers.

"I will come again and ask for another chart. Now Alys is two, perhaps you would draw up something which might tell us about her life?"

"I would be pleased to help," said Bennet. "Do call and we shall discuss it."

They parted and all the way home Bennet felt uneasy. He looked around carefully; was someone watching him? Was this the source of the feeling at the back of his neck. He rubbed it with the palm of his hand.

Once home, he went to the upper window to check the street. It was busy but there seemed to be no one watching the house. His feet absently took him into his workroom and he sat down to draw but his mind would not stay on the chart he was preparing.

Where was Christa? Ah yes, out at her marketing.

He wandered about the work room fingering first this chart and then that piece of equipment. He took the cloth from his master's armillary sphere on its plinth and studied it. It was a beautiful piece, originating, his master had said, in a far off place called Portugal and made of metal. Unlike the cheaper and less reliable wooden instruments this metal specimen was not prone to warping and so remained accurate. With this, Bennet could perfectly plot the positions of the sun and planets with respect to the horizon and the meridian.

He covered it over again and his eye lit upon a pile of parchments which had been 'filed away' by his master, if filed away was a word which could be used for such haphazard record keeping. This was certainly one skill in which Bennet excelled his master. He pulled them out from underneath his astrolabe.

He studied the charts of several people in the town and surrounding areas, many of whom he now knew were dead. He would dispense with them; get Christa to erase the ink with a pumice stone. He could then reuse the parchment, for this and ink was his biggest expense.

Here was the chart for little Alys Alleyn, who had come into the world in 1205 upon the day that Pope Innocent III had sadly stated that the Jews were doomed to perpetual servitude and subjugation owing to the crucifixion of Christ. That had been the 15th July and he remembered it well.

He absentmindedly took hold of it and sat at his work table to study it.

Here was a child whose character was of an intuitive and optimistic nature. She was destined to be greatly in tune with her own emotions and the emotions of others. Sun in Cancer, moon in Pisces, rising Leo. A virtuous and generous person, one who would be a force for good in her world.

Bennet began to draw more lines upon the chart and then, taking up an old piece of parchment which he had scrubbed, he began to progress the natal chart by two years until he reached early September 1207.

What he saw made him fearful. He threw it down onto the workbench.

"No! That can't be."

Words his wise master had spoken to him many years before when he had been a youth of thirteen or fourteen and just starting out on his apprenticeship came back to him.

"We may only see what we are allowed to see. We may not influence what is there, only reflect the truth of it. What will be...will be."

"No..." said Bennet to himself. "If we know beforehand what will happen, then surely we can influence it. Can we not turn that which is unfavourable to us into a situation in our favour?"

People came to Bennet for help in making decisions. Which day was the best day for a marriage? At what time should someone plan to make a journey? Which day was good for signing a contract? If he could tell them these things, why could he not tell them how to *avoid* something?

He locked the workroom; Christa would have no need to go in there. He scanned the street to see if he could see her coming back from her shopping. She was nowhere to be seen. Then he made a decision.

He washed his face in a laver of cold water and put on a new shirt. He had no idea why he did this, it just felt right, and then he went out into the street and locked the doors behind him. Christa must wait for him, for she did not have a key and there was no other entrance.

He threw himself into the hustle and bustle of the road as it was market day and the wide market place was full of stalls in a double row almost as far down as the church of St. Peter.

He dodged a cart with a cage in the back where sat a disconsolate pig and side stepped around a barefoot girl driving forward several geese with a long stick.

Now he was in the middle of the road. Looking round, he could not see Christa but then, in her new cotte of dull green brown, she blended into the throng very well. He might have difficulty spotting her in this crowd.

Returning a hello, from Master Cordwainer, Bennet nimbly skirted the back end of a horse who, lifting its tail, defecated into the road, and narrowly missing the lumps of dung, he stepped into the space by Chandler's Yard where swung a sign of the Golden Fleece.

He hurried on and ducked into Ironmonger's Lane, a lane quite narrow at its mouth and which widened at the top end where lay Back Lane. Houses and shops lined both sides. Here was quite a populous part of town with properties laid out higgle piggle, with the plots of gardens between.

A man came down the cobbled lane carrying a sack over his shoulder.

"Good man, where might Mistress Alleyn live?"

The man smiled a toothless grin. "She's the 'ouse with the pot o' parsley on the doorstep," he said laughing. "Thinks it brings her good luck."

Bennet laughed with him and pressed on up the slight slope.

Eventually he found the house. The main door did indeed have a pot of parsley outside it and he would never have found it but for that distinguishing feature, for its plot was narrow and almost only as wide as the door. He scratched on it hoping that the woman was in and called out. "Mistress Alleyn!"

A head appeared in the window above him and the woman shouted down.

"Who wants her?"

"It's Master Celest, the astrologer."

"Ah yes...wait..."

Moments later Bennet was ushered into a narrow hallway which opened out onto a room of about twelve feet square which housed both living space and kitchen as clean as a new pin and extremely tidy. The hall was open to the rafters and further rooms were to be seen through a door at the back.

"Mistress...I have come on a delicate matter. I know not what to do."

"Oh...do not fret Master Celest." The woman gestured to a stool. "I know you are a very busy man. I don't mind when you...or if you can't..."

"No, no, you don't understand." Celest sat and then bounced up again. "It's about little Alys."

"Oh bless you...she's with my mother at the moment."

"Where does your mother live?"

Mistress Alleyn's face was blank. "She lives by the barton at Barn Street."

"Ah...still in the town then."

"Yes...she's a Marlbury woman."

"Listen Mistress, I have had cause to look at Alys' chart today. I have no idea what made me pick it up. As you know, I drew up the chart in my apprenticeship, when Alys was born and my Master, God rest him, put it away. I found it today and looked at it and..."

The woman began to get agitated, moving her mouth around as if she'd speak but not knowing what to say.

"I did a little more work to it and...found that."

"Yes..."

"You must take Alys away from Marlborough, mistress; the month of August will be very bad for her. She..."

"Oh Lord above!"

"She is a fragile creature is she not...? With her lungs?"

"Aye she can be. In the winter she took ages to throw off a cough... despite all the remedies we could shove down her throat."

"She is a sun sign Cancer... the chest is vulnerable you see."

"So you are saying that she will be ill...?"

"No, Mistress.... I am saying that... that she will die."

Mistress Alleyn gave a shriek and stuffed her fists into her mouth. "No! Not my Alys."

"You must get her away. Right away somewhere else."

"But where?"

"Not in the town. There will be a contagion. Many folk will catch it and sadly, I think it will drive through the weak and the young and old like a forest fire. Alys will not survive it. She must get away."

"But where can we go?"

"Do you have relatives anywhere else?"

"What will my man think? Us leaving him like that?"

"If he loves his daughter, he will be glad for you to go," said Bennet quickly. "Is he here, let me speak to him?"

"No he's at work. He's the clerk, manager of scribes for Master Chapman, the clothier."

"Have you in-laws anywhere? Friends, where you can go for a while, just until the contagion is gone."

"My sister lives in Cadley."

"Not far enough."

"Is Ramsbury far enough?"

"Ah, that might do, I think."

"Then…" The woman grasped both of Bennet's hands, "We shall go to my Goodmother. She lives in Ramsbury. She works for the Lord there."

"Your husband's mother? That's excellent. And you must go soon."

"Oh Master Celest… you are a good man to come and tell me this," said the woman almost in tears.

"I cannot see little Alys suffer… I must say something."

"How much do I owe you…?"

"Nothing, nothing at all. My reward will be to see little Alys grow up to be a fine woman and the influence for good that she will be as she matures."

"Oh…" Mistress Alleyn picked up his hand and kissed it. "You are a *good* man."

"I… do… my best," said Bennet, a little embarrassed.

Out on the lane he felt a lot lighter, brighter. He had, he hoped, averted a disaster. Many would die, it was true but if he did not see their charts, he could not tell who would succumb and who would survive. He knew Alys, knew her when she was born. He could help *her*.

He swung himself onto the cobbles and began to tread down the lane.

He was so busy watching his feet, for here the way was not easy, the cobbles slick, that he did not look ahead until he was half way down the alley. Once he lifted his chin he noticed, at the end of the narrowest part of Ironmonger's Lane, was a dark shadow. The shadow of a standing man with a sturdy cudgel which he whacked into his hand suggestively.

The villain called John.

Bennet swore and turned up the lane hurrying up the cobbles; past the Alleyn's house again, up to the house of the parchment maker and ink seller. He rounded the overhanging thatch of the building when out from the side of a garden plot a few feet ahead, came two men also with cudgels.

A voice behind him shouted, "Astrologer! Hahaha. Didn't see *this* coming did you?"

*****

Bennet did not panic.

There were several ways out of this alley; if he could just get past the two men. Even if he took a blow, and he hoped it would not land on his head, he might safely be away.

He waited until the two came close and, casting a quick look backwards at the man called John, he fumbled in his purse.

"How much has he paid you to do his dirty work for him?"

They grinned nastily.

"Well...I shall pay you more to leave me alone," and he threw a handful of silver pennies into the air.

As he had expected the men dived for the money.

"Bastard!" shouted John and ran up the lane after him.

Bennet dodged past the scrabbling men and swung himself round a corner of a building which he knew had a long garden at the back. He picked up the hem of his long cotte and ran through the cobbled yard and then into a small orchard. He vaulted a low wall and, bending double, skirted it for a while until he came to a hedge. Damn! It was a hawthorn hedge and impenetrable. He looked back. Only the man John was following him and he seemed unsure where Bennet was hiding. Bennet turned and still bent double came back the way he had come. Reaching a gate he vaulted over it and ran up the hill, his lungs bursting. He was not a very physical man; he was a man who used his brain. He did not work out in the fields with his hands and was not used to physical labour; he soon tired. Again he looked back. No one was following. He stopped for a while to get his breath.

Bennet thought it best to try to reach Back Lane, for then he could get to any of the other small lanes which, each of them, ran back down to the marketplace; a market place which was full of people. It would be hard to whack him over the head with a cudgel in full view of a hundred people and get away with it! He ran on up the hill, puffing as the gradient became steeper and steeper.

Suddenly he was out at the lane which traversed the whole length of the town, parallel to the High Street. He was not alone here and that gave him strength. There were people around and about on their plots of land tending their crops. On he ran but a little slower now.

"Good Morning Master," said a woman he recognised but could not place. He nodded, for he had no breath with which to answer.

At last he reached the end of Chantry Lane. The slope was steep but down he ran, for this would bring him out almost opposite where he lived.

Off this lane were several yards where folk plied different trades. The candlemaker was here; and the man who imported furs from colder climes, had a repository here. Mistress Brewster had a large yard where she brewed her ale.

He passed the entrance to that yard and suddenly felt a sharp pain to the back of his head. He fell forward onto the cobbles and an excruciating pain went up his arm as his attacker hit his arm above the elbow with the cudgel and stamped three times on his right hand with a well-aimed and heavy boot. Bennet had not even had the time to yell. Even so there *was* a yell. He was sure he heard, "Oi! Get off him!" before he drifted into oblivion.

*****

It was only a matter of a few heartbeats and Bennet came to with Mistress Brewster peering at him concernedly and his friend Harry cradling his shoulders.

"We should get you home."

Harry tried to lift him but Bennet was still groggy and couldn't help him. "Bring him in to me for a moment," said the brewster, "He is still shocked."

Harry lifted him over his shoulder and together they got him into the woman's house.

"Did you see who it was?" asked Harry.

"Oh aye...I know who it is," said Bennet lifting a hand to his head. Mistress Brewster gently batted it away and put a cold wet cloth to the back of it.

"His name is John."

"That all? Just John?"

"I know him," said the alewife. "John Kydd. He's only been in the town a few months."

"And already he's made enemies," said Bennet. Then of course, he had to tell them, in embarrassed tones, the story of his near seduction.

"He was a kindling and faggot seller but obviously he thought he could make more money trying to defraud people and became a trickster," said the alewife.

"Mistress Brewster, do you know who the woman is? The woman who works with him?" asked Bennet.

"No...no I don't."

"Well, keep your eyes open. She is a beautiful creature but as sharp as a magpie's beak and as cold as frost."

"Though she can't be too cold, Ben, if she managed to stir your ardour..." said Harry laughing.

"Ah... no. She's as hot as Hell in that realm! I must admit it."

Harry took him under the arm. "Come on let's get you home."

*****

"Where the Hell have you...? Oh!" said Christa as she pushed off from the house wall. "What happened?"

"The man John attacked him," explained Harry. "The man called John Kydd?"

Bennet fumbled for his key and gave it to Christa. "You'll have to open it. I can't see straight nor use my hand."

They stumbled up the stairs and Bennet fell onto his pallet.

"Argh!"

"Oh no...look at your hand!" said Christa. "It's all bruised and puffy!"

"The man stamped on it," said Harry. "I think he knew that Ben is right handed and that it would make life difficult for him."

Christa fetched water and gently cleansed the back of Bennet's head. The blow had been glancing, for there was little blood but he would have a good egg on it for a while. His arm and hand were by far the most painful and debilitating wounds.

"Shall I go for the apothecary?" asked Harry. "He will tell you if it is broken."

"No...I think it is just badly mashed. But it will take a while to heal. For certain, I won't be writing or drawing for a while."

He lay down again and lapsed into a miserable sulk.

Harry made for the stairs. "You must let the town reeve know about this, Ben. The man attacked you. I'm your witness. Mistress Brewster saw him too. He must be apprehended for it."

"I'll think about it."

Christa began to bind up his hand.

"For goodness sake, stay out of trouble for a while," laughed his friend as he disappeared out of the front door.

Christa glowered at him under drawn brows. "So where did you go that you left me out in the street for a long time? What was so important?"

"It was important that's all. And I'm sorry. When the lockyer gets here, I'll get you a key so it won't happen again."

Bennet shuffled onto his side. "Now I need to rest."

"All right," said Christa in a huff. "I will make us some dinner."

But by the time she had sorted her shopping, Bennet was asleep.

CHAPTER SEVEN ~ REVENGE

Christa opened the door carefully the next day to find Harry standing on the doorstep."

"How is he today?" he asked as he came in stamping his boots. Ah yes, it was raining again.

"A little better though not much improved in his temper."

"Oh dear. Yes, he gets like that sometimes. How is his hand?"

"A mass of bruises but it's not broken. It is however numb from the thwack they gave him."

Harry bounded up the stairs.

"I thought I heard your voice," said Bennet.

"I have come to cheer you up!" said Harry.

"Humph."

"I have had some news from the town reeve today."

"Oh?" Bennet sat up straight and rubbed his sore arm.

"The man Basketwright has been apprehended."

Christa sat down on a stool and put her hands to her cheeks. "Oh thank Heavens!"

"It's not all good news though."

Harry drew a stool in between them.

"The man is lying his head off..."

"That's not a surprise," said Christa.

"He says that the reason he has been missing all this time is that he went up to Chippenham to try and find his wife. Oh no, he did not run away at all."

"But he can't have...I saw him in the street. Here."

"When he was told that his wife was found in the river not far from his cottage, he said that he wasn't anywhere near the town when she was dumped...whenever that was, and that it cannot have been him. *He* went looking for her because he felt uneasy."

"That's sheer nonsense," said Christa.

"The lad from the castle...Perkin... He said he saw him loading his cart," said Bennet. "What does he have to say about *that*?"

"He says that he loaded it with a view to taking it to market and changed his mind because he was so worried about Margaret, in the light of what the reeve had said. That's when he abandoned it and made off for Chippenham."

"He never did!" said Christa, "He came into town."

Harry shrugged. "Sadly they have no proof against him."

"But I..."

"I know. You saw him. But it isn't enough.

"Then why did he cut his hair and beard if it wasn't so he wouldn't be recognised?"

"Ah yes. The town reeve did ask him that. 'Is it a crime to cut one's hair nowadays?' he said."

"So, he's back at his cottage is he?" said Bennet.

"As far as I know, he is."

"Has anyone investigated the large basket which was on his cart?"

"Investigated?"

"For bloodstains?"

Harry shrugged. "I don't know."

Bennet took his lip in his teeth.

"And no...no. *You* are not going to investigate. You have already been in enough trouble," said Harry Glazer wagging his finger.

"He can't be allowed to get away with it, Harry," said Christa on the edge of tears.

"He killed my mistress."

"You know it, I know it...in fact I think the town reeve knows it... but we have no proof."

"Then how do we get it?"

Harry stood and flexed his considerable shoulders. "I think we must leave it for the present. These things have a way of working out."

"You have more faith in fate than I do," said Christa. "He is a bad man, giving out bad to people. Bad things don't happen to evil people like him."

Harry laid his hand on her shoulder and leaned over her. Bennet thought it was like looking at a giant and one of the 'goodpeople', so different in size were they.

"Let the town reeve deal with it. I am sure that Master Barbflet has some plan."

"He better had."

"Leave it Christa," said Harry. "I don't want to have found two women in the river!"

"Did *you* find her Harry?" said Bennet in a sadly surprised tone.

"Aye, I did. Just as you said. Before the castle mill, tangled in the reeds."

"Oh that's awful," Christa wiped her eyes with the back of her hand. "When will she be buried? I'd like to go."

"That will be up to her husband, now he's returned."

"Ah no...Christa. It's not a good idea for you to go," said Bennet. He will know you are in the town. At the moment he is unsure where you are."

Christa's chin came up. "I'm not afraid of him!"

"Now that *is* a change. Not long ago you were *very* afraid of him," said Bennet, with a sardonic smile.

Christa folded her arms. "That was then...this is now."

The men exchanged glances.

"Well, I had better go. This isn't getting shoes made is it?" said

Harry Glazer.

*****

They sat in a companionable silence when Harry left the house.

"Shall I go and bolt the door again?" said Christa at last.

"Yes. I won't be taking on any new clients for a while, will I? How can I? "He lifted his bandaged hand, "I can't even manage to do those charts for those people to whom I have already promised work."

Christa chewed the side of her mouth. "I could help."

Bennet looked up at her with a slightly mocking smile "Oh, and how could you do that?"

He chuckled to himself. 'Well, she is keen if a little naive.'

"You could tell me what to do and then check it afterwards. Watch me as I do it for you."

She interpreted his silence as agreement.

"We can begin in a while," She scurried off to lock the door.

"Now wait a moment," said Bennet as she returned, "I didn't agree to..."

"What do we need?"

"Are you sure your penmanship is up to it?"

"I am sure I can copy things with which I'm unfamiliar and I can write, after a fashion."

"And numbers?"

"Oh, numbers are easy..."

He watched her for a while as she tidied up the room, made his bed, cleared cups and washed them in a bowl.

She turned to see him laughing..."

"What?"

"I'll give you a silver penny for your enthusiasm!"

"Anything is better than you moping around here for days while your hand recovers and you can once again hold a pen," she said. "I don't think I could stand the petulant 'poor me...whatever am I going to do?' mood for much longer."

"I am not petulant..."

"Well you are certainly sulky and bad tempered."

"I am not."

He shifted on his chair. "I just hate not being busy. That's all."

"Then that is settled. Now, what do we do first?"

Christa proved quite able if slow. Bennet laughed at the childish way in which she pursed her lips in concentration, as she wrote the letters on the parchment.

"Now we need to do some calculating."

"I'm good at that."

"Oh...and where did you learn to be so good?"

"My father said I had a natural aptitude for figures and events and stories because I have the sort of memory which fixes them in my mind."

"Did he indeed?"

"Well, I could remember the Bible, all the stories in all the books, and where the lines appeared, and all the numbers of the lines. I counted them."

"Ah."

"No, it's true... I'll show you."

"Well, I have no Bible."

"Then, when we next go to church, I will ask Father Torold and I'll show you."

"Better still show me now."

And so Bennet read out the figures he needed to compute and Christa wrote them down and performed the tasks with which Bennet could plot the planets in the heavens.

"This table shows the motion of the Ascendant, at 55° north, during the course of a day."

"Ah..." said Christa completely lost.

Bennet chuckled to himself. "It has taken me seven years to learn this, Christa and I still do not know it all. I do not think one man can know it all in his lifetime."

He noticed that her cheeks had become hot and two red patches had appeared on them. He thought it quite appealing.

"Just look up the numbers and write them here and then we shall take some dinner."

"Has it stopped raining yet?"

Bennet looked out of the window. "No, still raining."

Christa wrote down very carefully, 6th hour 180.0 Libra.

"Good. After we have eaten I will...*we* will progress this and find out what will be happening in the mid-afternoon of that day."

As they ate their bread and cheese, Christa peered at the charts which Bennet had laid on the table.

"It's very complicated."

"It is."

"So how do you turn what is just a list of numbers and signs into a believable series of events?"

"Well… that takes a great deal of skill and a lot of it is memory. Not just *our* memory but those of all the astrologers who have gone before us. It's called interpretation."

"Was all this written down then?"

"Yes right back to the ancients. People have noticed through time, that certain things happen when particular planets do certain things and appear in different places in the heavens."

He realised that he was simplifying it for her so she would be able to understand it.

"For example, let's say the tenth house...which rules one's job," He pointed to a chart, "here...contains the planet Mercury and the sign Aries. Mercury, the planet of the intellect, and Aries, the sign of tempest, and when together, they show us a person with a sharp and zealous mind. Since they are both in the *tenth* house, this means the individual concerned will possess these characteristics in his professional life."

"Oh…"

"And when faced with certain difficult events in that life, will deal with them in a particular way."

"Head on, cleverly and bravely?"

"Exactly."

"And all these charts and numbers and squiggly signs tell you this, do they?"

"They do."

"This chart is for Master Metier. He's the Goldsmith…right?"

"Yes. He is a sun sign Capricorn and is good at making money. This chart tells us that shortly, he will have the opportunity to part with some of this money. Now he wishes to know if it is a good idea…"

"And you will tell him, yes it is, because…?"

"Because the person to whom he is giving this money as an investment will use it wisely and will easily return more than Master Metier has lent him."

"How do you know that?"

"Because I will also draw up a chart for that person and work out what he is likely to do too and compare them."

"Oh I see."

Christa sighed and dusted the crumbs from her cotte. "Oh why could you not just have been a farmer?"

"Ah but farmers too, need to know things…When to plant. When to reap."

"Oh."

"And I had not the opportunity to *be* a farmer. I was destined to be an astrologer."

Christa put her clasped hands in between her knees and leaned forward, chin up. "Oh I wonder what I am destined to do?"

"Be a wife and mother, I suppose. Most women are."

Christa eyed him suspiciously.

"You are only nineteen, Christa," said Bennet chuckling.

"I know plenty of girls who are married at nineteen."

"Most town girls marry a little older nowadays. And men even later and do not marry until they are sure they can provide for their chosen spouse and their family. Unless of course, they are marrying money."

"*I* will marry for love and nothing else."

Bennet laughed. "You have been listening to too many jongleurs' tales."

"My father loved my mother. They were inseparable and my father was destroyed when she died. He could not cope without her."

"That is very sad."

"And so I will wait until I find the right man; one that I can love."

"I wish you every success in your search."

"Now you are mocking me!"

"Not at all. You are young and hopeful. As we should all be at nineteen."

"And at twenty one?"

Bennet stood and took his cup to the pot board. He refilled it. "My master was a celibate aesthete. I will probably follow him along that road."

"That would be a pity because I am sure there are lots of girls who would find you very attractive."

Bennet's eyes widened.

"Not like that wanton woman...Ferret or whatever her name was. But, *really* think you are handsome and..."

Bennet cleared his throat. "Shall we get back to our work?"

*****

The day passed quickly and the evening grew darker and Christa lit some candles.

No more work was to be done in the gloom.

They sat and drank their last ale and heard in the quiet of the evening, the bells of the churches of the town ring for vespers.

Christa reached for her cloak.

"I think I will go to church. I haven't been since…"

"And I have not been either. Not since I buried my master."

"Then let us both go."

Christa's foot was on the second step.

"Ah wait. No. If we go, we must not be seen together."

"Why?"

"We have enemies, you and I."

"But if they wish us harm, that Ferret women and John Kydd know that I am here in *this* house."

"But Basketwright does not."

"He will not come to town...will he?" said Christa in a weak voice. "Surely he'll worship at Preshute. Mind you, he was never *at* that church. He is a Godless creature."

"I...I don't know."

Christa dithered. "Then I will go to church to pray for God's help. For surely we need it."

"You go...I will follow you."

And so it was decided.

*****

That night vespers was not so well attended at St. Mary's, for the torrential rain kept folk away.

Bennet stood at the very back of the nave, almost by the west door. Christa entered first and stood by a pillar half way up, almost hidden in a side aisle.

Bennet looked round under his eyelashes. There seemed to be no one here that he recognised as a threat to them.

A couple of older ladies had obviously come in together and were standing pressed close, their eyes down, their hands clasped in front of them.

Master Ash, the wheelwright and his three apprentices were

here. The woman who ran the glass business and her servants stood opposite Bennet in the other aisle.

He peered around a column. There was a small dark cloaked man and another thin individual whom Bennet believed lived up on St. Martin's.

He lifted a hand to Master Vyvyan Fuller, a town councillor, as the fuller entered the church and passed him, Bennet using the opportunity to check on Christa.

There she was, gazing at the small space visible through the arch where the priest was just beginning his Latin mass. The candles flickered, the space was quite dark.

Bennet did not keep his mind on vespers. His hand throbbed mercilessly and his brain was as foggy as a morning in November. Things went round and round in his head. Would he have to spend his life avoiding the felons who tried to dupe him of his money? Would Christa always be haunted by the presence of Master Basketwright? Was she really in danger?

At last he decided to ask God.

But God was rather busy and did not answer. Perhaps it would come to him later. Perhaps God would reveal what he intended at another time.

The service over, Christa passed Bennet and gave a little nod. Bennet slid behind her and walked a few feet in her train.

Vyvyan Fuller engaged him in chatter.

"Ah Master Astrologer, I hear that you were recently attacked in Chantry Lane? In broad daylight! What an awful thing? Do you know the culprit? Must we all be careful of our purses when out and about in the town now? Was it a theft?"

"No, Master Fuller, it was not a theft, it was a personal matter and I am beginning to heal. Thank you. But I must say I also had an attempt on my purse in the south porch here, a while ago.

"What is the town coming to?"

"I must hurry, the rain is slackening..."

The rain was not slackening at all. In fact it was getting worse. With darkness had come, straight down, solid sheets of rain blown by a gusty wind and the porch of the church was a funnel for the tempest which roared around the confined spaces about the buildings of Church Lane.

Bennet searched the darkness for the figure of Christa whom he could just see reeling in her cloak about her as it was buffeted by a gust stronger than any before. But it was not far to go to home.

For some reason he was uneasy. The weather was threatening; yes, the darkness unsettling, the night black, but this was more than a sum of these things. He looked behind him as he hurried through the alleyway and around the town cross. All he could see was the sheet of rain and the priest following in his dark cloak.

"Terrible night!" said Father Torold, passing Bennet with his long tread.

"Indeed, yes. I do hope we shall not have more flooding."

"Nor any damage to houses."

"We have had enough of it," answered Bennet as the good father peeled off down The Marsh.

"God be with you, Master Astrologer." His voice disappeared on the wind.

"And with you father."

Was Bennet always destined to be Master Astrologer? Had he no name of his own nowadays?

He pressed on. Now he could not see Christa...ah yes, there she was passing the entrance to Angel Yard, clasping her soaked cap to her head.

Suddenly the whiteness of it wheeled past him as another gust of wind completely took it from her head. He reached out to catch it but failed. It went bowling down the road back the way he'd come. He turned and pursued it.

It was then he heard the cry.

A cry for help... a panicked yell.

"Christa!"

He left the windblown cap and ran up the rain soaked road with its massive puddles and its uneven surfaces.

He jumped the gap between the houses on the High Street and the junction of Angel Yard.

The wind carried his voice away as he yelled, "Christa?"

"Ahhh."

He turned back. The voice came from a few yards into the lane. By the back door to the Green Man alehouse.

"Christa!"

If anything had happened to her, he would never forgive himself. Never!

He found her sprawled in the doorway of a hovel tucked into the wall of the wheelwright's yard.

He was soaked and dirtied so kneeling down was not going to make him any dirtier or wetter. He knelt.

"Are you hurt?"

He pulled out her cloak to look at her for damage. It was very dark just here and he could see very little

"No... no..."

"What happened?"

"My cap..."

"It's gone. We can get you another...or you can make one."

"My hair..."

"You're soaked. Let us get back into the dry. Home is but a few footsteps."

He lifted her up and wondered why she turned her face from him.

"Are you hurt?" he asked again, a little confused.

"No...no..."

He wrapped her soaked cloak around her and with her under his arm he cradled her body all the way to the front door of their house.

"I cannot deal with the key...here...you do it," he said, fiddling with his purse. His damaged and numbed fingers would not close around it.

"Here, you will have to get it."

She looked up at him with a glistening face, not, he was sure, just wet with the rain for her eyes were puffy and red and seemed to be full of tears.

She undid the purse...it seemed a personal thing to do; close up to him, her body pressed into his like a lover; groping at his belt as if it were an intimate matter. Eventually with a little sad cry she found the key and turned to insert it into the lock.

She gave a little scream.

"Christa...what is it?"

"No... not yet.. I'll tell you... later."

"Get in then... don't tarry."

"I'm doing my best!"

Another gust of wind took Bennet's cloak away and he grabbed it back. At that moment, he saw Christa's arm reach up to the door panel and pull something from its plank.

The door opened and she fell in.

He followed and pushed hard against the wind which buffeted the door. The key clicked in the lock, the locking bar went down.

Now he felt safe.

He turned. Christa had gone.

*****

He found her a moment later in her room crying pitifully into her hands, by the light of a single candle.

"It's not a problem. We might be able to recover your coif if when the wind dies down, we can search the street."

"No..."

"Well, we could at least try."

"No."

"Oh have it your own way."

He turned to go into his room and take off his sodden cotte and shoes, lifting down the curtain over the space which Christa occupied.

As he bent to undo his shoes, he caught sight of Christa rising from the bed and watched as she threw off her wet cloak. Something was odd.

Something wasn't right.

He knew that he should not be watching, but he did. Through the split at the edge of the curtain he saw her lift her dun coloured cotte above her head. Now she was dressed in her wet shift which moulded to the contours of her body. He saw the rise of her legs through the thin linen and the shadow of her breasts, small and neat, high on her chest as a young woman's should be. She lifted the shift over her head and turned her back to him.

He sat on the stool transfixed by the play of shadows across her skin. And still he felt uneasy. There was something wrong.

He stood abruptly.

"Christa...your hair!"

The girl grabbed a clean shift and pulled it to her body to hide her nakedness.

"You were spying..."

"No... no I wasn't. I promise. It's just... I knew something was wrong but I couldn't guess what until...I saw..."

Christa sobbed and with a deft movement threw the clean shift over her head. Then she picked up a blanket, wrapping it around her and pulled aside the curtain.

"What is it?" said Bennet.

She bent to a small stool which she used as a night table, the little table where the single candle in its chamber stick was perched.

Bennet searched around for the lamp and lit it. By the time he had the wick trimmed and the flame steady, Christa had come into his room.

In her hand she was holding a length of plaited material. A dark material.

"She said that my hair was longer and more lustrous than hers, and she could not have that."

Christa held up the long plait which she had worn down her back. Hair which had taken *years* to grow. It had been severed at her neck.

"I thought she was going to kill me..." she cried pitifully.

"Oh Jesu!" said Bennet, opening his arms. "Oh Christa."

Christa came pliantly into them and as his arms closed around her, her plait fell to the floor.

.

CHAPTER EIGHT
THE ALTERCATION~

Christa began to shiver with the shock.

"I thought she was going to plunge the shears into me," she said into Bennet's chest. "She dragged me into the alleyway and I thought she would kill me. But she cut off my hair instead."

Bennet cradled her in his arms. "It's because you threatened to do it to *her*."

"But I never would have done it... never! Not completely. It was just words... that's all. To frighten her off."

Christa's knees began to buckle and Bennet lifted her up.

"Come lie down for a little while." He led her to the bed. His master's bed. This bed which was big enough for the both of them. He must admit, he was tempted to lie beside her.

"Don't leave me." Christa grabbed him by the arm as he endeavoured to return to the main room.

"I...cannot...Christa, I can't..."

"I don't want to be alone yet... for a while... in the dark."

Bennet tried to pull away.

"Christa, it's alright, your hair will regrow." He watched her as she fingered what was left of her black locks. Her loose hair now only came to her chin. It was not even long enough to tie back. It had once almost reached the small of her back.

"She pinned it to the door. Did you see that she pinned my hair to the door?" said Christa in disbelief.

"Ah. That was what you recovered...how you found it?"

"If I hadn't found it, it would still be there for all to see...or the wind would have taken it away."

Bennet supposed that a young woman's hair was very important to her.

"Christa, it *will* grow again. It's not like she cut off your finger or something!"

"I didn't know what she was doing...I could feel her but it was so dark. She whispered into my ear. She *might* have chopped off my finger. Or cut my throat!"

Christa was still shivering.

"I will get you a hot drink of ale. Wait; it will warm you."

Bennet went to the small metal brazier upon which they did what little cooking they managed in the house and lit the charcoal. He nestled a pottery mug in the coals and blew on the flames. Then he poured in a measure of ale from the large jug sitting on the table.

Once warmed, he wrapped a rag around it and offered it to Christa. She sat up straight and accepted it.

"You think I am being foolish?"

"No, not foolish. It *has* been a... fearful experience."

"A girl's...a maiden's hair is...something precious to her."

"Ah... yes."

"My hair had never been cut in all my nineteen years."

"That is why it was so long? You were proud of it."

She took a swig of the ale and coughed. "I know that I am not a pretty girl..."

"Oh I wouldn't say that..."

"But I do know my hair was my best feature...and now it's gone."

Bennet rubbed his face with one hand. He was very tired.

"We shall see what we can do about it tomorrow."

She drained the pot and gave it back to him.

"Thank you. That has made me feel better, as you said it would."

He sat on the edge of the bed.

"We need to report this to Master Barbflet. It is a violation. An attack. A breach of the peace."

"You didn't report *your* attack and much more damage was done to *you*."

They sat in silence for a short while and listened to the wind roaring around the building, creaking and cracking the timbers, rattling the shutters and buffeting the roof.

Suddenly Bennet tensed.

"How did she know you had gone to church?"

"What?"

"How did the woman know you had gone out tonight? Was she simply waiting for you? I'd swear she wasn't *in* the church. She hadn't gone there and then simply noticed you were there also. She brought shears with her. She *planned* to do what she did."

He thought back to the meagre congregation at St. Mary's. Was there someone - this woman Ferrers, whom he'd missed, lurking in the church?

"It's not a night for going out just *in case* you might catch the person you're looking for, is it?"

"Was she watching?" asked Christa, her eyes wide. Bennet thought her short hair made her eyes look larger.

"If she was watching then she lives somewhere close by; somewhere she *can watch from*."

He went to fetch an old piece of old parchment and a graphite pen.

Grasping the pen in his bandaged fist, he drew the line of the street, both sides and then carefully drawing from the bottom by St. Peter's, he listed all those houses and businesses that he knew. Labouring the task, he wrote down the initials of the names of the people living there.

He didn't know them all and he found, to his surprise, that he didn't know who lived directly opposite them on the other side of the wide marketplace.

There was the house where Master Chandler had lived. Next to him was the old woman, the retired Mistress Sempster. Then on the corner, on one side of Chantry Lane in a house owned by Nicholas Barbflet, lived a bunch of grooms from the livery stable on the Marsh, all crowded into the small house. On the other side was the master Fletcher's house and business.

And then?

Who lived between the arrow maker and Mistress Sempster? Bennet realised that whoever they were they would have a good view of Bennet's front door.

Christa shuffled up on the bed. "What are you drawing?"

"The street. Do you know who lives here?" he pointed.

"In the narrow house with the tatty thatch? No."

"Then tomorrow, I shall go and knock loudly on the door."

"Oh no, Bennet!"

"They mustn't be allowed to get away with it."

Christa gave him an odd look.

"Then we must both report our attacks. And..."

"Yes...?"

"If you are out tomorrow, could you get me some linen so I can make another cap, please? I can't go out to my marketing looking like this."

"I'll have a search round for your old one."

"That would be kind, thank you."

But when he searched, he did not find it.

*****

As he lay down to sleep that night he realised that he had, yet again, failed to turn over the page of his little black book. Now he had two days to catch up on.

'You have made a grave mistake. One with which you will live for

104

the rest of your life and one you will never make again. The planets will punish you but you will come to see the justice in it.'

On the second page was written, 'Help will be needed today. Giving and receiving.'

Bennet stared at the short sentences. Mistake? What mistake?

He went to sleep with the word 'justice' ringing in his head.

Justice was also on his mind as he woke the next morning to find Christa already beetling about the house, with her broom and pail.

Once again he looked at her with her short hair and thought that she looked quite appealing with her hair swaying about her cheeks. The falling waves softened her expression and made her hazel eyes huge in her pale face. Her hair was usually severely scraped back from her face.

"There is ale already warmed," she said as she knelt on the steps to dust the stairs. No one had ever dusted the stairs with such vigour since Bennet had come to the house.

"Right." Bennet broke his fast with a piece of ale-dipped bread and pulled on his best grey cotte.

"I am going out to Master Barbflet. And I will get you some linen at the same time. How much will you need?"

"I was thinking that a yard will be alright, if it is wide. I can use the surplus for a headcloth."

"You'll cover your hair like a married woman?"

"When I go out, what choice do I have?"

Bennet lingered at the door. "I know that I said that there would be some remuneration involved in your staying here working as a servant and..."

"You have spent money on me already...there's no need."

"It is customary for a master to buy the livery of his servant or apprentice."

"Did your master buy your clothes?"

"Yes, he did. Did your mistress not do the same for you?"

"I was given her hand me downs. I had to take them up and in because I am... much smaller than she is...was."

"So the red kirtle...was not new to you?"

"No, she'd had had it a while. That is why it's a little faded. The master would not allow such further expense."

Bennet suddenly felt a pang of sadness.

He was half way out of the front door when he came back in.

"Christa, what is your favourite colour...do you have one?"

"Colour?" Christa had now taken hold of a small brush and begun to scrub the stairs with water.

"Well, I have never really thought about it..." She stopped and stared at nothing. "But I do like blue."

"The blue of a summer sky or the blue of a night sky?"

Christa stopped scrubbing again and dipped her brush. It dripped onto the step.

"The blue of the little harebells one finds on the downs about now."

"Ah...right."

By the time she had turned back to quiz him, he had gone.

She took out her anger at the state of her hair, upon the house. She scrubbed, rubbed, polished, swept and beat. Men did not understand the importance of a clean and tidy house. She would make sure that this house shone and sparkled. Bennet would have nothing to complain about.

*****

"So, you are telling me that this woman, whoever she is, waylaid your servant..."

"Christa Wren."

"Mistress Wren, and cut off her hair with a pair of shears?"

"Christa wore her hair in a long plait down her back, Master Barbflet. It was easy to snip off. Christa was afraid for her life when she saw the shears, for she thought she was about to be stabbed!"

"I'm sure it was very...frightening. Who is this woman?"

"She called herself Mistress Ferrers when she came to my house to ask me to draw up a horoscope for her but truly, I do not know her real name. She may have given me a false one. She is certainly a false woman."

"And you say that she has an accomplice who attacked you?"

"On Ironmonger's Lane. With two henchmen, though I think he had just found two disreputable men of the town and paid them to waylay me."

"There are such folk in Marlborough, sadly. No matter how hard we come down on them...another always seems to take their place."

"It is the way of the world, Master Barbflet."

"Why would he attack you?"

"Because he and this woman Ferrers tried to...hoodwink me and their ruse failed. I threw them out of the house."

"And damage was done to your arm and hand, you say?"

Bennet lifted his bad arm and bandaged hand.

"I have two witnesses, Mistress Brewster, who says the man is called John Kydd and Harry Glazer who saw everything which..."

"Ah yes. Two respectable town dwellers. We know this man Kydd. He is a troublemaker. Though we have never been able to pin him down to any particular house."

"I wonder if, at least the woman who associated with him, lives next to Master Fletschier."

"You have seen her?"

"No, but... she must have been able to see *us* from where she lives, in order to trail Christa last evening. And that is the only house which has not been occupied for a long time. I can't say who lives there now. Our house is very visible from there."

Master Barbflet wrote down the position of the house.

"Right when my men are free I'll send them to the house to see who we have there."

"Let *me* go, sir."

"I'm not sure you should young Bennet..." He put his hand on Bennet's arm to turn him to the door. "Leave it to us."

"Thank you, sir."

Bennet walked back to his front door. He stood for a long time staring across the street at the narrow house with the tatty thatch.

Then, making up his mind he marched across the road, stood in front of the house and giving a cursory glance to his own front door - yes it was very visible - he kicked the door panel.

"Kydd...you in there?"

There was no answer.

"Kydd if you are there, or your mistress in crime, just to let you know, I have reported you both to the town authorities. You'll be getting a visit soon."

Message delivered, he was about to march back across the road when a heavy hand pressed onto his shoulder.

"Master Astrologer," said an oily voice, "I'd not stand under there if I were you. That thatch is very dangerous."

Bennet looked up into the threatening eyes of John Kydd, who pushed him onto the wall and held him there. Bennet wriggled.

"Let go!"

The man did not let go but pushed even harder. "I can't be responsible for what might happen, *Master Astrologer*, if the whole lot came down on your head."

He reached up and grabbed a handful of the deteriorating straw thatch and pulled it. A lump came falling down upon Bennet's head and wisps of mouldy straw floated on the breeze.

"Of course, it's not *my* house. So it would be nothing to do with me if you were injured. I only rent it from the Widow Partridge."

"Your threats don't frighten me, Kydd."

"Oh but they should. I never make a threat without I carry it through...*Master Astrologer*."

Bennet threw off Kydd's hand. "Enjoy yourself in the lockup, Kydd," he said as he pushed off the wall.

Kydd grabbed him again and there was an undignified tussle where the felon tried to punch Bennet.

Bennet's strength, not to mention his grip with such an injured arm and hand was certainly not superior to that of Master Kydd and he almost fell but as he teetered, his foot connected with the leg of the man holding him. It caught the weak spot at the back of the man's knee. Over went Kydd, cursing and swearing.

Bennet was quite surprised at the result, for he had not envisaged himself getting the better of the man.

"And stay down," he said, moving backwards across the road, "or it will go badly for you."

The woman from the house next door poked her head from her window.

"Oi! You."

Bennet looked up.

"Stay away from us or else," he yelled to Kydd and continued across the street.

Kydd jumped up but he skidded on the wet thatch which he'd pulled down and once more was brought to his knees swearing.

Bennet was safely through the traffic, across the road and into the mercer's close by Figgins Lane before the man could right himself.

"Master Mercer, good day. I am wondering if you have a fine wool in a blue colour."

"Blue...we have plenty of blues, Master Celest."

"Might you have..." Bennet fingered his earlobe rather self-consciously, "one that's the colour of a harebell?"

"Ah...I see..." said the cloth merchant with a smile as big as a cloudless sky.

Pointing to a bale, "you mean...like this...?" he said.

"That's perfect. Um... how much might I be needing for a lady's cotte? For my servant, you understand."

"This is rather good quality, sir, for a servant."

"That is of no matter."

"Well then, you'll need three and a quarter yards. At this width."

"Then that is what we shall have. Oh and some nice linen for a coif. Have you that too?"

"Master Celest...we have everything," said Master Mercer, reaching for his shears.

*****

Bennet called out as he re-entered the house.

"Christa, you upstairs?"

"No, I'm here."

She came out of the workroom with a broom in her hands.

"You haven't touched…"

"No, nothing. Only swept the floor But truly, the place needs a good clean."

Bennet chuckled. "I don't think it's had that in seven years or more."

"Well, I'll do it but only when you are here to tell me what to do."

"Here, I have something for you." He held out the linen keeping the wool behind his back.

"Oh yes, linen, thank you very much. I'll cut it out later and begin to sew it…" She wiped her hands on her hessian apron and took it, laying it on the table.

"And this…" He stretched out his hand.

Bennet would never forget the ecstatic look of joy on Christa's face as he handed her the blue wool and indeed, he never forgot it to the end of his life.

Two spots of red appeared on her cheeks. Tears welled up in her eyes. She grinned as wide as the High Street and gave a little cough before bursting into tears.

"Oh! That was why you asked me about colour."

Bennet's face dropped… "You don't like it? Have I got the wrong colour?"

"No... no. It's just right!" She brought the piece of fabric up to her cheek and lovingly caressed it.

"It's perfect. No one has ever bought me..." She leapt forward and Bennet was taken unawares as she curled her arms around his waist and embraced him.

"Thank you. Thank you."

"Well... now you can have a really nice kirtle to go to church in."

Christa drew back. "It's beautiful. But how will I make it? I have no thread or shears. I could pull thread from the linen to sew a coif and I have a needle in my things but this requires something more."

"Now I know what it is what you want, I can go and get some thread from Mistress Sempster. And shears from Master Cutler."

"You'd do that?"

"Of course I will..."

"You are the kindest of men, Master Celest," she said, wiping the tears from her eyes. "I have never known a kinder nor thoughtful man."

"Not your father?"

"He was kind and gentle, yes, but a little..."

"A little..?"

"Otherworldly. He did not understand the world as you do."

"Oh Christa, I do not understand the world...I think no one but God can do that. I just stumble along."

"No, you are kind and thoughtful and very clever. I do not know a cleverer man."

"Steady now. I will not get through the door for my head swelling," he chuckled. And changing the subject said,

"Let it never be said that a servant of mine had not a good kirtle in which to go to church to praise God."

Christa watched him carefully. It seemed to him that in that look there was a little disappointment.

He cleared his throat.

"Let's have some ale to celebrate and then I will go out and get you some shears."

*****

Bennet had gone and Christa sat for a while finishing her ale and staring at the blue cloth which she'd laid on the table.

She was not lying when she'd said that no one had ever given her anything so wonderful in her whole life.

Her entire nineteen years had been lived in relative poverty. Her father had not been a wealthy priest. Her life with the basket maker's wife had been hard and frugal, partly because basket making, whilst a good trade, did not pay enough to keep any of them in luxury, owing to the Basketwright's propensity to drink away much of the profit. Margaret had only taken Christa into her house because she had been a friend of her mother's before her marriage to that cleric, and when she'd heard that Christa had been orphaned she offered to help. The basket maker, however, would only have her, if she worked for her keep. And so Christa worked.

And now she worked for a master astrologer, who it seemed was a relatively wealthy man. He owned a house of his own, and all the equipment needed to do his job; equipment and books which were not of little cost or value. He had very good furniture in the house. A grand bed and fine linen sheets, thick woollen blankets and household equipment, pottery, fine cooking equipment and a brazier. And he could afford to spend money on expensive cloth for his new servant.

She realised that this was a purchase which was designed to bolster his standing in the community, for if his servant was seen to be well dressed then, it would be known in the town that the man was successful. And that was good for business, wasn't it?

That thought left her feeling a little empty; she didn't know why.

Bennet was soon returned with a pair of large shears for Christa to cut out her cotte. She set to straight away, laying the blue wool out on the newly swept and scrubbed floor.

Bennet went back to work with his computations. He could just about manage a graphite pen with his right hand but after a while his hand began to ache with the pressure required to write, and so half way through the afternoon he wandered up the stairs to see how Christa was getting on.

He watched her from the top step. She was bending over on her knees and pinning the pieces of fabric together with some veil pins. Things were obviously not going well for she tutted and muttered under her breath.

"How do you know where to cut?" he said suddenly and Christa surprised, jumped with a little "Oh!"

"I'm sorry; I didn't mean to startle you."

Christa struggled up from the floor. "I laid the cloth doubled on the floor with the fold at the top…"

"Yes?"

"Then I lay down on it."

"Oh?"

"And measured my length on it from the neck where the fold is. Then I folded it where my ankle came. I added a bit for the hem…"

"That's clever."

"Then I cut straight down."

"And then across?"

"Yes. And then The material which is left I divided into two triangles. These are for the gores...here."

On the dress she was wearing, she lifted her arm and showed Bennet where the pieces fitted.

"This allows movement of the arm. And then I cut the sleeves."

"Have you done this before?"

"No, but I have seen it done several times."

He came up into the room. "I wouldn't have the confidence to cut it."

She grinned at him. "If I want a new cotte, I must make a new cotte."

"Why were you muttering?"

"Oh I don't really have enough pins to keep it all together."

"Where can they be had?"

"A cutler or a sempster - they have them."

"I am in need of a walk around. I'll get a bad neck if I hunch over my work too long. I'll go and get you some pins and have a walk along the river to clear my head and stretch my..."

Christa gazed at him, "Neck?"

He chuckled. "Legs."

"That would be really kind, thank you. It will make things very much easier. And I am sure they will come in handy in the future."

As he clomped down the stairs, Bennet laughingly called up, "I foresee it!"

Christa ran to the window and watched him as he left the house, locked the door and turned up the High Street, disappearing at last when he reached the fifth house from their own along the road. She leaned out as far as she could to see him, but he had gone down one of the small lanes between the houses, which led to the river.

Sighing, she returned to her cotte and, taking up the linen which Bennet had bought to make a coif, she pulled some threads from the warp of the piece with which to baste her woollen kirtle together.

Bennet had been gone quite a long time when she realised that, although the basting together of the pieces could be achieved with this thread, it wouldn't really suffice for sewing the wool.

She picked up her cut out and tacked together kirtle and laid it across her bed. Then she sat by the window, in the light and began to sew the hem of the linen headcloth. Her coif could wait.

She was half way round when Bennet returned.

"Did you enjoy your walk? You've been gone quite a long time."

Bennet shrugged his cloak from his shoulders. "It's beginning to rain again, only lightly but..."

"Shall I close the shutters?"

"But you need the light."

"It doesn't matter."

"Here...some pins and at the same time, I bought some thread for you to sew your kirtle."

He threw her a small wooden spool and she deftly caught it.

"Oh you remembered?"

"I hope it's the right thing. Mistress Sempster said it was what you'd need." He tousled his damp hair.. "Well... I suppose I had better get back to work."

"Can you manage with your bad hand?"

"In short bursts. I can't sit almost all day at it, like I would normally do."

"Do you want me to come and help you again?"

"You have sewing to do."

Christa put her linen on the table, "I can do that at any time."

"But it's better done in the daylight, isn't it?"

She chuckled. "Daylight... yes. Not this half-light we have at the moment."

"It's been a dull old day."

They sat down together in the workroom but hardly had time to take out a pen when there was a voice at the outer door.

"Master Celest?"

Bennet looked out of the window.

"Master Lockyer...I will be but a moment."

The master locksmith greeted Bennet and they fell to talking about the new and improved lock which the astrologer wanted fixing to the door.

"It's a sturdy door, Master Celest, not easy to break into unlike some."

"My master Geoffrey had a lock fitted many years ago but I feel that surely now there are better and more advanced contraptions available."

"There are indeed. I would advise..." And at that Christa lost interest.

Her eyes scanned the table where Bennet had left a few charts. How she wished she could interpret them.

One which was uppermost took her attention.

'Alys Alleyn born in 1205 upon the fifteenth of July. Sun in Cancer, moon in Pisces, rising Leo,' read Christa out loud but under her breath. 'She is barely two.'

Christa followed the words with her fingers and tried to understand where the symbols belonged upon the circular chart of the little girl's natal day.

"Here is Venus...I think. And here is...is that one Jupiter? Ah yes it is."

The voices of the locksmith and the astrologer diminished as they went out into the street to look at the outside of the door.

"And this is the first house or the ascendant. That governs the physical health..."

"And a new and stronger lock upon the strong box I have in the house, please John."

"I can bring one and fit it here. And perhaps we should think about securing it to the floor?"

Voices diminished again and once more Christa looked out of the window. John Lockyer and Bennet were shaking hands upon their business.

No sooner had Lockyer gone, had Bennet closed the door and was half way across the room, than a vicious kick was delivered to the panel of the wood.

"Master Celest. Open up. The town reeve wishes a word with you."

Bennet sighed, turned back and opened the door again.

"Why is there the need to kick in my door Jonas Pike? A polite call is all that's needed to get me to open it. What's the matter?"

Pike didn't seem at all worried about his rudeness. "Like I say, the town reeve wants a word with you."

"All right. I will be along presently."

"Now!"

Bennet would not be bullied.

"See here, Jonas. I'm a busy man. I can't just drop..."

"My instructions are to bring you to him...now! No delay. No excuses. Now."

"Why is there all this great hurry?"

"Master Barbflet doesn't want things to get... out of hand."

"What do you mean out of hand?" said Bennet crossly "

"If you are going to be difficult, I can go and get help..." said Pike, leaning backwards from the doorstep and eyeing another of the reeve's townsman who was at that moment coming up the roadside.

"Hey, Pearson. He won't come..."

"I haven't said I won't come, man!" said Bennet with real irritation in his voice. "I will come...wait till I get my cloak, it's raining."

"Ah no... and have you run out the back and over the wall?"

Jonas Pike laid a sturdy and calloused hand upon Bennet's arm. His bad arm.

Bennet threw him off with a pained intake of breath.

Now the town reeve's man angrily grabbed Bennet by the shoulder. His bad shoulder.

"Whatever is the matter? Master Pike...isn't it?" said Christa coming out of the workroom, with Bennet's cloak in her hands, smiling and fluttering her eyelashes.

The miller's man was taken aback and released Bennet for a heartbeat.

"Ah mistress..." he stared at Christa's hair.

"Why must Master Celest be dragged away so unceremoniously?"

Jonas Pike gave Bennet a nasty grin.

"He's wanted in connection with the murder of a man called Kydd, that's why. John Kydd."

Christa took in a surprised breath. "Murder?"

"Aye, now are you coming or shall I have to drag you?"

CHAPTER NINE ~ THE PLAIT

"Murder?" said Bennet, totally surprised. "You say that Kydd is dead?"

Master Barbflet motioned for Bennet to sit on a stool placed before his table in his office at the town corn mill.

"He was found today, an hour before nones, floating in the river at the back of our mill."

Master Celest stared into space with puzzlement.

"You last saw him...when?"

Bennet swallowed. "I saw him outside his house on the High shortly after I last spoke to you, sir."

"Outside his house?"

"I must admit that I confronted him and told him that I had reported his actions and those of his accomplice to you. That you would shortly be asking him some telling questions."

"Even though I had asked you not to approach him," said the town reeve with a grim expression.

Bennet hung his head. "That was all I said, whereupon he attacked me."

"Again?"

"I managed to get away and went straight into the shop of Master Mercer, across the road. Please...ask him. He will tell you when I was there and what I purchased."

"And then?"

"I walked home. My servant will verify that I was there then."

"Mistress…" Nicholas Barbflet thought for a moment. "Christa Wren."

"That is correct."

"She's outside, sir," said Greaves, the miller's man. "She insisted on following Master Celest here."

"Then let's have her in, William."

William Greaves nodded and opened the door.

"So, that was the last you saw of the man?"

"It was."

"You have a known grudge against this Kydd and his accomplice; this woman with whom you say he works a particular trick; a ruse upon men in the town."

"Have no others lost money to these two? How many have fallen for the charms of this woman only to be fleeced of their savings or takings? This man Kydd wanted money from me so that he would not spread the gossip around town that I had raped his wife," said Bennet.

"Raped his wife?" said Greaves, bringing in Christa and closing the door. "Jesus."

"It was a complete lie," said Christa.

"Thank you mistress, we shall ask you about this in due course," said Greaves holding onto her arm and keeping her away from Bennet.

Master Barbflet grimaced. "Thank you Greaves, you can go now."

Christa shook off the red faced miller's employee and came to stand by Bennet.

"I want to know what happened then?" asked the town reeve.

Both Christa and Bennet began to speak at once but with a sidelong look from her master, Christa subsided into mutters.

"I worked in my workroom all afternoon until I went to the sempster's to buy some thread.

"Thread?"

"For me..." said Christa quietly.

Having previously bought some shears from Master Cutler," added Bennet.

"Shears you say?"

"They were for me too," said Christa in a small voice.

Nicholas Barbflet took in a huge breath.

"Shears?"

"I couldn't cut out my wool unless I had some shears, sir. Master Celest kindly went out to buy them for there was nothing in the house good enough. Or sharp enough," said Christa with a little more confidence.

"The man Kydd was found in the river but he did not die from drowning."

Bennet and Christa exchanged worried glances.

"He had been stabbed in the back with a large sharp blade."

"A large...sharp...blade?"

"Like a pair of shears?"

"It certainly looks like it could be a wound inflicted with such a weapon," said Barbflet.

Bennet folded his arms defensively in front of him. "Are there no others in the town who have a need to want to be rid of this tiresome Kydd?"

"I have no doubt there are...several," said Master Barbflet, mimicking Bennet's folded arms. "But only one was actually seen threatening him."

Bennet dropped his arms.

"Threatening?"

"Mistress Kitchener. She lives in the house next door but one. She swears she saw you shortly before the man was fished out of the River Kennet, arguing in the street with Kydd."

"Yeees... I did, as I told you. But I left him alive and went shopping for fabric at Master Mercer's."

Nicholas Barbflet sighed again, rose from his table and shouted out through the door. "Greaves... go down to the Mercer's - ask if he has seen Master Celest today and what time that might have been."

"Yessir." The outer door slammed.

"So you went home. And then worked for a while."

"He gets a bad neck with too much leaning over, you see," said Christa.

Barbflet pushed a stool in her direction and she sat.

"And he went for a walk in town and I saw him go to the sempster's where he bought me some thread."

"How long did this take you?"

Bennet opened his mouth to speak.

"He wasn't gone long," interrupted Christa. "And he was on the street the whole time."

Bennet gave a quick nervous twitch like the movement of a bird and looked at her from the corner of his eye.

"So you can see the sempster's house from your window Mistress Wren?"

Christa flushed. "No...not completely. But I can see it from the road."

"You were in the road?"

"I...was... in the road looking at the door. The master had just decided to ask the lockyer to come and change the bolts of the front door and I was looking at the old ones, trying to imagine..."

"Imagine?"

"Imagine how a better bolt and lock might improve the safety of the house."

"It's true, Master Barbflet. John Lockyer had just been to see us and we discussed the replacements shortly before Pike dragged me here."

Nicholas rubbed his temples.

"You argued with the man Kydd. You left him. Where did he go then?"

"I have no idea," said Bennet.

"He attacked you. You fought him off."

"No weapons were drawn."

"You left him; you went to the mercer's and cutler's and then home."

"That's correct."

"And then a little while later you went to Mistress Sempster's shop?"

"Yes. But I did not see John Kydd again and I did not kill him, with or without a pair of shears."

Nicholas Barbflet's eyes flicked from one to the other.

"Sir, might I say that the shears which my master brought home; they had no blood upon them. Go now to the house and seek them out. I left them on the floor of the upper room. They are clean."

"They are easy to cleanse."

"But I would surely have seen the blood on them when he brought them home, if he had been guilty of the murder?"

"Unless of course the *two* of *you*..."

"No!" they both shouted. "We are not killers," said Bennet.

Nicholas Barbflet scrutinised Christa's hair. She had left it free and wore nothing over it because she had so quickly left the house after her master had been accosted by the town reeve's man. She pushed it self-consciously behind her ears.

"She made a good job of it didn't she?" he said with a slight tone of sympathy. "Your hair."

Christa blushed and ran her fingers over her crown.

"You must believe us, sir," said Bennet.

"We have been together the whole day...except for when Master Celest came to you, went to the mercer's and cutler's and then to the sempster's," added Christa. "When I saw him."

Nicholas Barbflet played with a stylus which was on his table. He twirled it in and out of his fingers.

"It seems this man Kydd was a blessed nuisance. I shan't be sad he's gone but...it's still murder and I must report it to the coroner. And to the Constable of the county, Sir Aumary Belvoir."

"That is the law, sir," said Bennet nodding. 'We are ready to defend ourselves in front of anyone you choose."

"I have known you, Bennet, a long time. You and your master. I am inclined to believe in your innocence. Therefore I am going to let you go. I will put in a good word for you with both constable and coroner. I know them both personally. I know that you will be able to prove your worthiness as a member of your tithing. There will be many folk who will attest to your good character."

"Thank you sir."

Christa stood up. "Can we go now, sir? The house is unlocked you see."

Greaves came back puffing and simply nodded.

"It seems the mercer has provided you with an alibi, Bennet."

"Thank you, sir."

"For goodness sake, keep out of trouble Master Astrologer!"

Out in the open air, Bennet looked askance at Christa. "What was that about stretching my neck?"

"Legs...you went to stretch your legs."

"Hmmm. And I've managed to avoid having my neck stretched. For the moment."

They walked home slowly.

"Christa...?"

"Yes?"

"Tell me, why did you lie?"

*****

She had not immediately answered him and so when he'd closed their house door behind him, he asked her again.

"It was a lie. You couldn't see me all the time. Why did you lie?"

Christa gave a huge sigh.

"What is it to you that I lied?" Her wild eyes were fixed on him.

"Why do you think I lied?"

"Do you lie so easily?" He had not meant it to come out so forcefully but it had and there was no unsaying it.

Two red spots appeared on Christa's cheeks.

"I lied for you. You went out to walk by the river. You were away a long time. What do you think Master Reeve will make of that?"

Bennet huffed.

"And can you tell *me* truthfully that you did not kill this man Kydd?"

"Christa!"

"Well, can you?"

Bennet was so absolutely taken aback, he was unable to answer.

"I might also ask, can *you* lie so easily?" and she flounced up the stairs with a toss of her short hair.

Bennet went back into his work room and slammed the door. He took up his graphite pen and attempted to write and do some calculations but his hand was cramping at every stroke.

"Christa!" he yelled up the stairs from the doorway. "Can you come and help?"

Eventually there was a disgruntled clomping down the stairs and Christa came into view with several pins stuck into the breast of her dun cotte.

"I'm sorry to interrupt your sewing but I can't seem to write even as well as I did this morning."

Christa tutted and sat down.

They spent a short while, Bennet dictating and Christa scribing and eventually the atmosphere became less frosty.

"And the presence of Mercury in the tenth house…"

Bennet threw down the parchment he'd been studying, pinching the bridge of his nose.

"Christa…you can't really think that I would have anything to do with killing a man? No matter how awful that man was."

Christa looked up from her writing. "No. I don't think that you

125

could kill anyone in cold blood."

"But you think I could do it...on the spur of the moment with my blood up?"

"You have a bow. You can kill things with a bow."

"Rabbits and..."

They looked suspiciously at each other for a heartbeat or two.

"Do you really think that I killed Kydd?" asked Bennet.

"No. I don't. And you know why I lied to the town reeve. If I had told him that you'd said you were going down to the river, I don't think you'd be sitting there now. I think you'd be in the town lock up charged with murder."

Bennet pursed his lips.

"But lying Christa?"

"Sometimes...it's just something we have to do."

"You will have to make confession..."

"Next time I see a priest, I will."

Bennet sat thinking for a while. She had lied to protect him. But of course it was for her own good too. If he was arrested and found guilty then Christa would be homeless and rootless again.

He took up his parchment once more. "...and Mercury in the tenth house indicates..."

"That the person will be a good teacher," said Christa with a smile.

Bennet looked up. "You have been studying?"

"I told you, I have a good memory."

Bennet's stomach grumbled. "I think we shall eat early and then..."

"Then what?"

"It's a full moon tonight. Let's go up onto the common and I will show you the positions of the stars in the heavens. It will be very clear tonight, I think."

Christa began to get the food together prior to cooking on the little brazier in the upstairs room.

She called down, "Master Celest?"

"Bennet."

"Who *do* you think killed the man John Kydd?"

The astrologer reached for another piece of parchment to read.

"Perhaps another man they had tried to blackmail."

"Or a woman?"

"Yes, I suppose it could have been a woman."

After a short while a delicious smell began to waft down the stairs. Bennet left his work, locked the door and followed his nose.

"It might even have been the woman who called herself Ferrers," he said. "I have no doubt she would kill him if he became troublesome to her."

He picked up the plait which Christa had laid on the window ledge.

"Christa, why have you laid your hair here?"

She lifted the spoon with which she was stirring the stew and took a little sip.

"There is a tale about the Goddess Sif, wife of the Norse God Thor. She lost her beautiful long fair hair when the mischievous God Loki cut it off as she slept. He was so worried about what he had done, he had dwarves make a replica in real gold and so when Loki presented the new gold tresses to Sif, Thor's anger was appeased."

"But why put it here?"

"There is a legend that if you put hair into a window it may be restored to your head, by the dwarves."

"They do this for mere mortals do they?" said Bennet with a slight smirk.

"You never know," said Christa.

*****

The sky was a huge expanse of dark blue above them as they came out at the top of Back Lane by the common.

Bennet reached for Christa's hand and pulled her up the steeper slope onto the very top of the grassy area overlooking the town. They were both out of breath when they reached the summit. A few lights in the town twinkled below them. Hundreds and thousands of lights twinkled above them.

Bennet fell down on the grass and stared up. It was still a little damp but he didn't care.

Christa followed him, a little more circumspect.

"How big is the sky, Bennet?" she asked. "I know it is probably a silly question but no one has ever told me how big it is."

"How big?" Bennet chuckled. "We do not know how big it is. But the astronomers tell us that the planets which we study are many, many miles away from us. And they are spinning around us. Some believe that the sky is a huge celestial bowl upon which the stars are fixed."

"That is why the sun moves in the sky?"

"That's correct. The sun and all the other bodies are moving around us."

"Then where is it now?"

"Below the horizon...somewhere else. In other countries," he said. "Those who have travelled great distances tell us that the sun rises in the lower half of the earth's sky as it sets in our sky."

Christa tried to come to terms with the enormity of it.

"It's just not possible to count all the stars, is it?"

"No. Only God knows how many stars he has made in the heavens."

Christa giggled. "It's odd. When I look at the bigger stars I can see others out of the corner of my eye. But when I try to look at *them*, they disappear."

"There are clusters of stars which can only be seen in this way." Bennet pointed up to a bright star almost above them.

"But that, that is Venus, a very bright planet."

"The planet which governs love, isn't it?"

"Venus governs our sentiments, what we value, and the pleasure we take in life. It is a little simplistic to say she only governs love."

"Ah."

"And that is The Great Bear."

"Oh I read that in your book. 'Ursa Major,'" said Christa, picking a grass stalk and digging her teeth into the sweet white root of it.

"Indeed. Do you remember what the bear does?"

"I do. Ptolemy said that astrologically both Ursa Major and Minor presage an evil influence. They are particularly injurious as regards the affairs of nations and kings." She quoted from a book which Bennet had lent her.

"You're right, you do have a good memory."

Christa felt light headed with Bennet's praise.

"What's that one?"

"That is Andromeda, the chained maiden."

He felt her look at him in the dark, wanting more of an explanation.

"Andromeda is named for the daughter of Cassiopeia in the stories of the Greeks, who was chained to a rock to be eaten by a sea monster."

"Oh no!"

"But she was saved by Perseus the hero... Don't worry. And of course he fell in love with her and married her."

"So it has a happy ending, this story?"

"Well...more or less. Andromeda makes up part of the astrological sign of Pisces." Bennet pointed once more.

"How do you know where they all are? There are so many of them."

"Night after night. Sitting here listening to my master as you are listening to me. And days and days of study looking at maps of the heavens."

Bennet stretched out his arm. "Eventually it all went into my head."

He felt for the cool sheep and rabbit cropped grass under his fingers and pulled up a couple of stalks. Absently he began to plait them into a braid. Not very well because of his injury.

He reached out again and plucked a few more.

Christa came up onto her elbow. "Do you think a girl could learn all these things?"

"I am sure a girl could learn them but it will take her longer..."

"Why?"

"Because she has work to do about the house as well as learn and study."

Christa giggled and lay down again. Now she was a little bit closer to him and he felt the warmth of her body.

He reached out for more grass and found her hand.

She did not pull it away and he left his hand resting on hers. Somehow it felt... good. They lay in silence for a long while.

"How often do you come up here? she asked at last.

"As often as the sky is clear and the planets can be seen, though lately I have not been up here at all. There have been other things to do."

"Now I am here, you will have time to do much more," said Christa. "Maybe you will be able to come up here more often."

"We should go. It is getting chilly. And we must be in before curfew."

He leapt up and offered his hand and she reached up grinning, to take it.

Hand in hand, his good hand, they ran down the hill.

Back in the warmth of the house, Bennet realised that he had brought home the plaited grasses he'd made on the hill. He stared at it and then gave a glance to the plait of Christa's hair, lying on the small window ledge.

He picked it up.

"Christa, come here a moment."

"Why?"

"I want to look at your hair."

"Why?"

"I have an idea."

She came slowly into the room puzzled by his request.

"Sit here a moment. I am going to try something."

Slowly Christa sat on the stool.

"Now lift your chin."

Owing to his bad hand he was rather ham-fisted in his efforts; Bennet teased out a few of the strands of the long plait of hair which was secured at the very bottom with a tight band of thread.

Slowly he began to take the short tresses of Christa's cut hair and twine it tightly into the free ends he'd pulled out of the plait.

"It's working but, I think I can probably do it better with practice."

"What are you doing?"

"Hush and keep still."

He was half way across to the nape of her neck when she spoke again.

"Are you mending my hair?"

"I'm trying to weave the cut hair into the hair left on your head. I had the idea that it might be possible when we were up on the common tonight and I was plaiting stalks of grass."

"Oh."

His hand touched the back of her neck and she shivered.

"Sorry…"

"No...no… it feels...nice."

Bennet went on plaiting and weaving.

"I expect a woman who is more used to weaving could do it better."

"Maybe I shall ask the lady across the road. She used to be a sempstress. I hear she is very good at making braids and band weavings."

"Well, that would be a good idea."

The night was quite old when they finished.

Bennet took hold of the completed plait and gave it a tug. It held but it could have been more secure and tidier.

"It will be a little shorter than you are accustomed to, but I think it will do."

Christa gave Bennet a look he could not fathom and then lifted herself onto her toes. Pulling him down to her by his chin, she kissed his lips gently, once.

"You are a kind and gentle man," she said. "Thank you."

CHAPTER TEN ~ THE SPELL

They were both very tired that night and retired as soon as they could. Bennet watched Christa pull the curtain over the alcove which made up her private space. Then he dug under his mattress and fetched out his master's book.

'You will avoid a dangerous situation today but that danger is not yet past. Concentrate on your work and do not allow yourself to be deflected from your purpose.' His master gave him no indication of what that purpose was.

He looked over at the faint glow creeping from under the curtain. Christa had not yet extinguished her candle. He blew out his own light and settled on his side to sleep, his arm aching badly.

Christa lay staring up at the rafters listening to Bennet's easy breathing. She was planning on doing some washing tomorrow; Bennet had told her that it would be a fair day for such a thing. She would go out to the river and see if she could find out where the man Kydd had been thrown in. Then she would take some time to approach the old woman, Mistress Sempster and see if her plait could be tidied. She closed her eyes and tried to sleep but, even though she was tired, a vision of her poor mistress, Margaret Basketwright, kept intruding into her thoughts. She banished those notions and then in their place came a body floating in the river. She blew out her candle and stared into the total darkness.

Now into her mind's eye came a picture of Master Bennet Celest.

A man of middle height and weight with brown wavy hair parted to the centre, falling past a high soft skinned forehead to a sharp chin. His eyes were the grey blue of the little pond she had seen in the forest. She imagined his hands. Long thin fingers, with a palm as small as a girl's. Now of course, one of those hands was wrapped in a bandage. They weren't working hands; these were the hands of an academic.

She imagined her own hands. For her small size, *her* hands were large, sturdy fingered and strong and the skin on them was calloused and rough. She rubbed her hands together in the dark. They made a rasping sound. Her own hands were working hands.

An awful feeling constricted the area of her heart.

He would never look at her in the way in which he had stared at that woman, Ferrers. Even if she was a liar and evil, Bennet had been attracted to her. She was beautiful, there was no doubt.

And Christa? Christa sobbed to herself. She was plain, small with no real attributes. Her hair had been, as she'd said, her only asset. And now. She tugged on it. It held. She tugged again in frustration and it began to come away from the weaving which Bennet had achieved.

She sobbed for a long time, until she cried herself to sleep.

*****

It was, as Bennet had predicted, a perfect day for washing and Christa wrapped the bed sheets and pillivers in an outer sheet and took them down to the river where she pummeled them against the river stones and scrubbed and soaked them until the anger she'd felt at losing her hair was diminished.

In its place was an empty feeling of loneliness and loss. It was then rapidly replaced by curiosity.

She dragged the linen up to a clean part of the bank and began to squeeze the water from it. It took her some time. Half way through the operation, to give her hands a rest, she scanned the area for people and left her washing. Making sure there was no one watching, she ran down to the back by the corn mill to see what she might find.

She could see that there had been a few feet treading the bank; it was muddied and churned. She looked out over the water - nothing particularly to see there. She scanned the bank closely, the grasses and plants. Nothing out of the ordinary presented itself. Her cotte was wet. There was no way that she could do the washing in this way without becoming very wet herself. She took off her shoes and waded out to one of the culverstones, placed in the bed of the river to indicate the depth of the water. She leapt from one culverstone to another, for just here there were three. Standing in the middle of the river she stared down its length. Something glistened in the water.

"Ah mistress," said a voice behind her. "The water is hardly deep enough to take you away just there. You'd be better off in the mill pond, if you are thinking of self-harm."

Christa turned slowly.

"It's good enough for washing."

"Ah... that's what you're doing." The man looked round chuckling. "Where's your linen then?"

"Over there."

"What're you doing here, then?"

Christa thought quickly, "I wondered if it might be easier to do it here...than there." She indicated the bank where she had been working.

"Aw no...you don't wanna be doing it there."

"Oh?"

"That's where a man was killed."

"Oh my!" said Christa, quickly thanking the stars for the opportunity to talk to this man. Whoever he was.

"Who was that then?"

"A man called Kydd. Not a Marlbury man. Only here a while."

"What happened to him? Did he fall and drown?"

"Aw no... he was murdered. Fell right there."

"Oh how awful."

She scanned the river where the man pointed. "How do you know all this."

"I work for the miller. I saw the body float past."

"Terrible."

"Aye it was. And then a few of us came out and dragged him from the water. He was already dead of a slice in the back."

"Was there anyone else here?" Christa tried to seem a little disinterested but desperately wanted to know what the man knew.

"Ah no. We didn't see who did it. But there's some talk that it was the town astrologer."

"Ah no... I don't think that can be right," said Christa authoritatively. "I heard at the market that he was elsewhere when it happened."

"Ah right..." The man narrowed his eyes. "You know about it then?"

"Not much, only a little."

"Right." The man stared at her.

"Well I had better be getting back to my washing."

"Yeah...yeah...you do that."

Christa waded to the bank again and began to wring out her sheets.

The man followed her.

"Not often we see nice young ladies out here."

"Oh?"

"What happened to your hair?"

"Oh...that." She tossed her short locks as if they were still long. "I have had a disease. I was very ill. Sadly I lost it all but... It's growing back now."

The man's eyes grew large. "A disease...?"

"Yes. It's terrible. All your hair falls out. Apparently it's very... catching." Christa began to walk towards him.

The man backed off.

"Well, I'll leave you to your ...washing then."

"Yes."

The man ran off. As he ran, he fingered his long wavy dark blond hair.

One look back and he was gone around the corner of the town mill.

Christa laughed, dropped her washing again and once more waded into the river. At the second culverstone, she bent and plunged her hand into the water to her elbow.

Out from the pebbly depths, water streaming from her sleeve, came a shiny object. Relatively new and well sized, it was of quite a complicated design and Christa fixed her eyes on it.

"Well what have we here?"

She turned it over. "Ah yes. I know what *this* is." She smiled to herself.

"Master Bennet will need to see this."

*****

Christa hoisted the washing to drip and dry onto a makeshift wooden contraption in the backyard of the house and then went in to change her dress and dry off.

She placed the little silver object on Bennet's table with a click.

"Recognise this?"

Bennet stretched and lifted his hands above his head, yawning.

"What is it?" He picked it up. "Should I know what it is?"

"You *have* seen it before."

His brow frowned. "Where did you find it?"

"In the middle of the river at the back of the mill by the big stones."

"The culverstones?"

"Where the man Kydd met his end."

"Ah we don't actually know…"

"Oh yes we do, because I have spoken to one of the men who

dragged him out of the water."

Bennet looked puzzled.

"I was at the river doing the washing when I met him."

"Ah yes, of course. Well, why should I know it? Did it belong to Kydd?"

Christa picked up the small pendant. "It's an ampulla which was filled with the holy water of Canterbury..."

"Yes, I can see now that it's an ampulla."

"A badge of the Blessed Saint Thomas, whose mementos are often shaped like sword tips."

"Yes, it's certainly a sword...and what does it say....?" He turned the little thing around in his fingers, "'COMPVSA OPTMVS EGORVM MEDICVS FIT - Thomas is the best healer of the worthy sick.' How do you know about it?" said Bennet sitting back in disbelief. It seemed that he was often going to be surprised by the knowledge of this young woman.

"I have seen it before." The little ampulla showed a picture of Thomas Becket Archbishop of Canterbury wearing his mitre.

"Have *you* been on..."

"No, but my mistress had. She had been to Canterbury to pray to Saint Thomas to intercede with God to make her well."

"There can't be too many of these in the town."

"Canterbury is a popular destination...and this may not be the only one of these in Marlborough but..." Christa turned it over. "there is a dent in it. I know that dent. I saw the little thing get damaged."

Bennet swivelled on his stool.

"You saw? How?"

"My mistress went to Canterbury with a party from Marlborough, to ask for the saint to intercede, make her well and allow her to conceive a child. I didn't go as I had to stay with the master to look after him while she was gone. When she returned, she had this thing dangling from her neck on a thong."

"That's how you know it?"

"I know it because when she came home with it, the master was angry and struck her saying that she had no business buying a gewgaw such as this with his hard earned money. The little thing buckled and flattened and when it was straightened again, it bore the crease which you see in it here."

"Then your mistress must have lost it..."

"Ah no."

"No?"

"She was wearing it on her dress the day she died - do you not remember it on her when we came to visit you?"

"Now you mention it..."

"And where else have you seen it... because we both have. More recently."

Bennet stood up abruptly in surprise.

"God's little fishes! Mistress Ferrers..."

"You think she has been to Canterbury?"

"She had one just like it round her neck when..."

"It was not one just like it...it was this very one. I have put this often enough around Margaret Basketwright's neck to know it well."

"I don't understand," said Bennet.

"I saw it but it didn't register at the time. However it was this very one for I saw the crease in it."

"Then how?"

Christa shrugged. "There can only be one answer."

Bennet's face turned slowly to hers.

"Ferrers stole it from the body of your mistress?"

Christa sat down quickly on Bennet's stool... "How about...my master gave it to Ferrers after taking it from his wife's body?"

Bennet blinked in confusion.

"Did they know each other? Ferrers and Basketwright."

"You know what they say?"

"Hmm?"

"One felon knows another..." said Christa.

*****

"Oh you poor girl. Whatever happened?"

Mistress Sempster invited Christa into her house and bade her sit in the light.

"It was an accident. My friend and I were larking around and...it accidentally got chopped off."

Christa wasn't going to tell her the truth. That was far too complicated.

"My master, the astrologer..."

"Master Bennet...yes, a lovely lad."

"Yes...I think so too. Though he's not a lad any longer."

"Ah no... a master now."

"He suggested that I come to see you, to see if you might make it whole again. He had a go at repairing it but he isn't a person who is used to weaving."

"And of course you can't reach," said Joan Sempster, fingering the black locks left at the nape of Christa's neck.

"No."

"Well, let me see what I can do." She chuckled. "I've been asked to make some things in my time but, never replace a severed plait. That will teach you not to lark about with sharp objects. Think what might have happened..."

"Ah yes indeed."

The sempstress began to part the hair into several strands, asking Christa to hold a few of them back.

"I think the best thing we might do is plait from a higher place on your head than you would normally wear it. That way we have more of the hair you have left, to work with."

Christa could see nothing and left the woman to work in silence. After a while Mistress Sempster asked Christa to let go of the hair she held back.

Then as the woman plaited, Christa asked questions.

"Your neighbour, Mistress Joan?"

"Which side dear?"

"There. That side."

"Ah yes...?"

"She has beautiful hair doesn't she?"

Joan stopped plaiting. "I don't believe I have ever seen her hair. She keeps it covered as a good married woman should." She picked up again.

"Oh, she's married?"

"Yes. To a soldier I believe...or someone like that."

Soldiers were not usually married but it was not unknown.

"I am sure I've seen her with her hair flowing free like a maiden. It's long and wavy and beautifully blonde."

"Oh I don't think it can have been her, dear."

"Does her husband work at the castle?"

"I have no idea. They haven't been here very long and to be honest I haven't had much opportunity to talk to her. She keeps herself very much to her house. Though of course, it's not *her* house, it's Mistress Partridge's. She owns a lot of houses in the town which she rents out."

"Yes, that's what I'd heard."

Joan plaited on.

"You say she stays at home. She doesn't spin or weave at home for any master in the town?"

"Not as far as I know but as I say I don't know her well."

"Well she managed to get herself a very handsome, well set up man."

"Ah yes. I have seen him, Master Kydd."

"Oh how I wish I could get myself a handsome and well to do man."

Mistress Sempster stopped plaiting.

"You do?"

"Oh yes. I like working for Master Celest but...it means I am just a servant. I would love to get married and be my own mistress and have children and…"

"It's very overrated you know."

"What is?"

"Marriage."

"Oh…I thought…"

"But you're young and are bound to be looking around for a handsome face and a well-shaped leg. It's the way of youth."

Christa looked askance at the woman. "I am? Oh yes…of course…I *am*."

"Have you anyone in mind, my dear? It always pays to have someone in mind."

"In mind…?"

"A man with whom you'd like to become… you know…better acquainted?"

The woman carried on plaiting. She was now getting to the end of her work.

"I have some thread here somewhere. Ah yes. That will do nicely." She threaded some blue thread through a large eyed needle and wound it several times tightly around the end of the plait and passed the needle through the hair a few times.

"Now let's see what that looks like and see if it holds." She gave it a sturdy tug.

"Ow!" said Christa, not expecting it to be so secure.

"You must wash just the head and the plait, you can't undo it or you'll have to start all over again."

"Yes I realise that."

"And tie it up when you sleep or wear a coif. It will come undone if you aren't careful with it. I have no idea how long it will last but…"

"Thank you so much Mistress Sempster. I have no money to give you but the next time I make a bag pudding, can I give you one?"

"That would be lovely."

Christa rose to leave.

"And can I give you a little bit of advice?" said the woman.

"Oh...wha...what's that?"

"If you would draw a good husband to you, then..." The woman looked over her shoulder but Christa could see that there was no one else in the house.

"Then..." she came closer."

"Take a candle and set it in a dish of water. Into that water..." the woman whispered "put the tip of your fingernail and a little blood from a finger."

"Oh...?"

"And sit in total silence until the candle goes down and is extinguished by the water. Whilst you sit, think about the person you would like to fall in love with you. Say their name in your head, over and over and ask them to come to you."

"You don't have to speak it?"

"Aw no. Just *think* about it."

Christa rehearsed it in her head. "Bennet Celest, come to me."

"Then you may throw away the water and the rest. And soon after you will meet your lover and they will be very attracted to you."

Christa made for the outer door. "A candle...would a stub do?"

"Oh yes, as long as it's a flame and you are best to stare into the flame for as long as you can."

"Thank you Mistress Sempster. Thank you for everything."

*****

That night, as Bennet slept in his corner by the stairs, Christa took a small candle stub about two inches tall and placed it into a dish of water. She sat on the floor, carefully pared her little fingernail into the dish and gritting her teeth, stuck her sewing needle into her index finger three times and allowed the blood to drip into the water. She watched in the half light as the red swirled around the candle stub whilst the light from the wick flickered and wavered.

Sucking her finger she prepared for a lengthy wait.

Christa wrapped a blanket around her shoulders, set her shift tightly around her cold feet and drawing her knees up to her chin, she spoke inside her head.

"Bennet Celest, master astrologer..." Best to make sure of the person. There was no one else in her life called Bennet and certainly no other astrologers in the town. "Bennet Celest come to me. Bennet Celest come to me. Bennet Celest come to me."

She could not count the number of times she had said this before, Bennet stirring in his sleep muttered something, which to Christa, seemed very much like a garbled version of her name. Her heart started to beat faster.

She began her spell again. "Bennet Celest come to me."

Over and over, she rehearsed his name and stared at the little flame as it hovered above the wax like the glow worms she had once seen out towards Preshute.

"Bennet Celest come to me."

She had not realised that she had spoken aloud.

"Christa?"

Panicking, Christa did not want to end the spell but keeping her eyes on the flame she called out "It's all right. I am reading one of your parchments."

That would account for him hearing her voice, for she was like most reading folk, and could not read quietly in her head.

"Sleep well," she said.

She continued her litany. Over and over. Her eyes began to fail her and she blinked. The candle flame was still steady and unwavering.

"Master Celest...ah no... Bennet Celest, master astrologer come to me." It was getting more difficult to concentrate.

'I wonder how many times I will have to perform this spell?' she thought, in between the words in her brain.

Eventually after fighting her nodding head and her falling eyelids for a while, Christa gave in, and fell asleep leaning on the end of her bed.

In the middle of the night, when it was extremely dark, she was woken by a scratching on the outer door downstairs. She listened carefully. Her right leg had gone numb and she rubbed it until the feeling disappeared.

"Oh help me God. Have I conjured up a demon? Is he trying to get into the house?"

She scrabbled on all fours to the window and on her knees, peered through the small gap in the shutters, onto the street below.

A dark shadow was just moving away along the roadway. She watched until the figure drifted from her view towards St. Peter's.

Bennet slumbered on.

She stood up and tiptoed from her room, across the floor and down the stairs, carrying her dish and the spent candle.

All was dark. Everything was in its place.

She left the dish by the back door and once more looking carefully at the front door, as she passed, she tripped lightly up the steps again. It was nothing. She thought the shadow was probably one of the night watchmen employed by the town reeve to keep the curfew and patrol the town for miscreants at night.

Feeling satisfied with her night's work, she donned her newly made coif, pushed her mended plait into it, lay down and slept until dawn.

*****

The next morning, Bennet found the note which had been pinned to the outer door, when he stepped out to look at the weather before delivering a chart to a client who lived on Silver Street.

He pulled it from a nail.

"What's this Christa?"

He gave it into her hand and she unfolded it.

'I know where you are. I am watching you,' it said.

❧   *****

"Can she write?"

"She can certainly read a little, or at least she led us to *believe* she could," said Bennet, pulling on a dark blue surcoat. "Ferrers scrutinised the chart I cast for her, as if she could understand at least some of the words on it."

"But Bennet… the shadow I saw didn't seem like a woman to me."

"It's hard to tell in the pitch black looking through a gap in a shutter, let's be honest."

"Why is she taking things to such extremes," said Christa in a perplexed tone. "She could have killed me the night she cut off my hair. If that is what she wishes to do...why, tell me, she is stalking me now?"

"She is enjoying tormenting you."

Bennet put on his boots.

"Where are you going?"

"To the town reeve, with this message."

"What can he do?"

"He might be able to apprehend her in her house and ask her a few questions."

"To which she will lie and there is no doubt she will use her womanly charms on anyone he sends."

"I am not letting this go."

"Why not?"

"You...*we* cannot spend the rest of our lives worrying about what she is doing."

Christa suddenly had a thought. "Do you think she knows that I found the ampulla? Was she watching then? Is that why she is so angry, for I can... can tie her to the death of that man Kydd?"

"I don't know." Bennet came close to her and took her shoulders in his hands. Her heart gave a little skip.

"I cannot have you in danger. If anything happened to you, I

146

would never forgive myself."

Christa's heart gave another little skip.

"Stay here and bolt the door..."

"Oh no. I am coming with you. I don't want to stay here alone."

Bennet hesitated. "Oh all right."

They locked the outer door and Christa could not help but give a glance towards the house with the tatty thatch across the road. Hurrying along, she took a brief look all around her. Few people were out so early.

"Mistress washerwoman! Did you manage to get your washing dry?" said a voice behind her as they wandered into the court by the millpond. They'd been told that Master Barbflet was in the mill building.

Christa turned to see the friendly face of the blond headed mill worker she'd met at the river.

"I did, thank you."

Bennet ducked through the door of the mill and disappeared inside. Christa was about to follow when the young man stepped in front of her.

"What's your name then?"

"Christa."

"That's a very pretty name," he said smiling, as he blocked the doorway. " A pretty name for a pretty lady. That the astrologer you were with?"

Christa licked her lips. "Yes. He's my master."

"Thought you said that..."

"Yes, well I didn't like to say yesterday."

The man craned his neck to look at her plait.

"My goodness. Your hair has grown enormously quickly."

"Yes, yes it has." Christa tried to push past the man but he wasn't for budging.

"How did you get it to grow again? Overnight?"

"Ah...I erm... I know a little magic."

The man's eyes bulged in his head. "Magic?"

"Magic...to make hair grow and other things."

"Comes of living with an astrologer does it?"

"Er...no...now excuse me."

The man leaned over her, "what other things do you know about then?"

Christa was tempted to stand on his toes but she stepped away from him.

"Oh you'd be surprised."

"C'mon then. Ol' Ben isn't easily shocked,"

"Ben? Ben is your name?"

"That's right Ben, short for..."

Christa clamped her jaw shut. No, let it not be Bennet.

"Benedict."

Christa let out a huge breath. "I have to go in now."

"Aw. no...not when we are just getting ... acquainted."

"I am sorry, Master Benedict but I have no desire to become acquainted with you. Now if you'll let me pass?"

His face took on a wounded look. "Well that's nice I'm sure."

"I have to go to my master."

"Well then...see you around." He stepped away from the door. Christa pushed past him and as she drew level she felt him pinch her bottom.

"Something to remember me by," he whispered in her ear. And sauntered off whistling.

Christa quickly caught up with Bennet by following his voice to the back of the mill building where Master Barbflet had his office.

"You do not have any idea who put it there?" she heard the town reeve say.

"Someone who wants to frighten."

Bennet caught her eye and his expression said, 'where have you been?'

"Master Barbflet," said Christa, "I saw the dark figure of a man walking away from the house shortly after the...incident."

"It was a man? The astrologer here believes it to be a woman."

"With all due respect, my master did not see the person."

Barbflet looked from one to the other.

"And this was found at the site of the murder of the man Kydd," said Bennet giving over the little ampulla.

"What is it?"

Christa looked to Bennet for her clue.

"It's an ampulla of holy water from Canterbury. My mistress, Basketwright's wife who was murdered, brought it back from pilgrimage. I recognised it."

"You...recognised it?"

"It belonged to Margaret. See here the small dent and crease in it. I was there when the little thing was damaged. That's how I know."

Barbflet turned it over in his fingers. "How *do* you know?"

"I was there when Master Basketwright struck her, damaging it. He struck her in exactly the same way that time as he struck her when she died."

Bennet took up the tale. "We wondered if there is a connection between the basket maker and the woman called Ferrers, for when she came to my house to consult me that day, she was wearing this."

"Even though it didn't belong to her," added Christa.

"And that puts the woman, Ferrers at the river when Kydd was killed," said Bennet lifting his chin confidently.

"Basketwright and Ferrers must have known each other before my mistress' death."

Nicholas Barbflet sat down on his chair and leaned on the arms.

"This is a very...complicated story."

"Nonetheless what we tell you is the truth."

"Oh...I have no doubt that the truth lies somewhere in the story."

Christa took in a hurried breath to interrupt. "I have it from the woman who lives next door to her that Ferrers pretends to be a married woman but when she came to Master Celest's house, she was bare headed and her hair was free flowing like a maiden."

This mention of hair reminded the master miller of Christa's predicament with her own hair and he gave it a good look.

"Ah...your hair is restored I see?"

"The sempstress re-plaited it for me. It's a temporary repair," said Christa shuffling her feet. "That's how I knew about the woman Ferrers."

Barbflet grunted down his nose. "All right. I'll send a party to the house and get her to come here. If she is guilty of anything, I'll have it out of her."

Out in the courtyard again, Christa and Bennet looked at each other in dismay.

"He doesn't believe us," said Bennet.

"He'll do nothing."

"We are on our own Christa," said Bennet folding his arms.

CHAPTER ELEVEN ~ HUNTED!

A little while later there was a scratch on the door.
"Master Celest!"

"What now…?" said Bennet bad temperedly. "Will I never get any work done?"

It was Jonas Pike, now far less belligerent than he had been but with an air of angry disappointment.

"My master wants you to know that he sent us up to the house of the woman you called Ferrers."

"Oh yes…good. And?"

Christa came up behind Bennet and peered around his shoulder.

"He wants me to tell you that the woman is no longer there. The bird has flown. The house is empty."

"I hope that she's flown the town. She's probably mined the seam that was the ready money in the town. She won't be able to work her trick without her partner anyway. Thank you Master Pike."

Jonas Pike looked bewildered.

Then Master Celest shut the door on him.

Bennet and Christa stood transfixed.

"Where has she gone?" said Christa.

Bennet took hold of her shoulder with a firm hand. "Wherever she's gone, she isn't here and she can't hurt you. That's one good thing."

"I'm not so sure. She might just have moved somewhere locally."

"Well, if she is still here somewhere in the town, she will be seen by someone. Word will get round. We must keep our eyes open."

"Could we ask a few folk to help us? To keep their eyes open too."

"I could ask Harry," said Bennet. "He sees a lot of people in the town and knows them well."

"We mustn't let down our guard until we know we are truly safe and she's gone."

Christa squared her shoulders. "She's not going to stop me living life normally."

"That's the way," said Bennet, pecking Christa on the cheek. "What say we have some ale to celebrate?"

Christa gently rubbed the spot where he had kissed her. He had *kissed* her! The spell was working!

*****

Bennet went back to work and picked up the chart upon which he'd been performing calculations but he couldn't concentrate.

'Since Christa Wren has come into my life, I have hardly done any work! What is it about her?'

He read a line of his workings.

'Scorpio and Virgo are deeply compatible signs. These signs are both very intellectual and both value friendship and connection, making it easy to open up to one another. This bond has the potential to be as intimate as can be."

Bennet had not been assessing the compatibility of their *own* two signs; the chart he worked on was, coincidentally, comparing the compatibility of signs which were identical to Christa's and his own. In the course of his work, he had come across a parchment upon which his master had written. He realised that it had been the basis for the entry in the little black book which he'd read the night before last.

'You have met your intellectual equal. Your friendship will

blossom, though it will be fragile at first."

He tossed the parchment onto the table and picked up the work he had been intending to do before being interrupted by the miller's man; Master Glover's chart. Glover, a Scorpio, was intending to marry a much younger woman, a Virgo, and he needed to know if that marriage was one based upon trust and affection or simply upon financial gain on the part of the woman. For the elderly glover there was no doubt it was pure lust.

Bennet began to transcribe his findings, very slowly with his injured fingers. But his mind was not on the subject.

He was worried. It was true. The last entry in the little black book, that which he had read last night, bothered him.

'The danger is not past. There has been a transformation. What seems to be, is not. What is, seems not to be.'

His master always had had a fondness for obscurity.

"Oh don't beat about the bush Bennet,' he said to himself, 'just tell Master Glover that things will work out and be done with it. Then pass on to other things.'

He sat back and sighed. "But what was he to do about Christa?"

He looked out of the window and saw Harry approaching the house through the marketing crowds. Jumping up, he hollered through the window, "Harry...a word?"

He saw Harry lift his hand and hurried out to open the door for him.

Harry was surprised when he'd heard the whole story.

"And so now the woman is gone from the house, maybe from the town and yet you still feel that she is a malevolent presence here?"

"Both Christa and I do."

"Where is Christa by the way?"

"Christa? Out at the market. She is trying not to let the situation change what she does and how she does it."

"She has courage, that one."

"Yes...and that's the other thing."

"What?"

"I engaged her as a servant."

Bennet realised that Christa had been an excellent servant to him. He had no complaints. The house had never been so clean and tidy. His meals had never been so well cooked or frequent. His clothes had never been so well kept.

"But?"

"She is becoming more than that."

"You are beginning..."

"No...I don't think...well...yes, maybe. I know that she is becoming very fond of *me*."

"And you are not...?"

"I don't know."

"Well then, all you can do is see what happens."

Bennet folded his arms across his chest. "That is your advice is it?" Harry grinned.

"And you and your Gunilla? That's what you did? You lived in the same house."

"*She* is my master's daughter. Things were a little different for us. You are your own master. You say how things are conducted."

"Do you think I should say anything?"

"At this time. Probably not. Just keep going the way you have been going. But keep a tight rein on yourself." Harry wagged a finger. Bennet knew what he meant.

"All right." Bennet sighed, "all right I shall."

"And yes, I'll keep my ear to the ground and my eye sharpened. If I hear that the woman Ferrers as much as breathes in Marlborough, I'll let you know about it."

"Thank you. You are a good friend."

As Harry left on his way to work, clapping him comradely on the back,

Bennet's eyes chanced to stray across the marketplace, where he saw Christa in her old red cotte, her basket over her elbow. Her black plait was an arrow, an arrow with a little kink in it, down her back. Not as long as it was when he first saw her, it's true, but still long and beautiful.

He watched as she was approached by that man who'd been hanging around outside the mill that morning.

Ah so this was the fellow who she'd met whilst at the washing at the river. He was tall and shapely with broad muscled shoulders and strong arms. Wasn't that what every girl desired? His long golden hair shimmered in the sunlight. They were laughing. Christa was throwing back her head and chuckling at something the young man had said. He touched her on the arm. She did not pull away. She leaned in and whispered something in his ear.

Now it was his turn to say something. Bennet could read his lips. "NO?" the man had said, in incredulity.

Christa nodded and then with a toss of her head she turned about, waved at the man and was gone from view behind the cabbage seller's stall.

'Perhaps I am wrong,' said Bennet to himself. 'I am reading things wrongly. She is not overly fond of me. Only as a servant is fond of a master.'

He felt foolish and went back to work.

That night he almost dared not open his little book. He sat for an age on his bed and stared at it.

"Oh this is silly," he said aloud and thumbed through the pages already read.

'You are now entering a time of quiet and peace. Take time to rest and think and build strength There will be nothing happening for weeks. Then you will need endurance.'

"What?"

Bennet hesitated and then, contrary to his master's instructions, he turned another page.

It was empty. Nothing was written upon the vellum except the date.

*****

Bennet turned page after page for days. Nothing had been written. He did not dare come to the end of the blank pages and so only turned one a day, as instructed.

The daily routine carried on. Christa cleaned, cooked and marketed in the mornings and helped Bennet with his work in the afternoons, scribing for him. His hand eventually began to mend.

Christa's transcribing became quicker, he noticed, and now and again she almost anticipated what he was about to say, smiling sweetly when she had got something right. That smile made his heart twitch and he had to smile back.

One day in September, when the swallows were massing on the chandler's roof and the starlings were wheeling in the sky, Bennet was looking for the stubs of the candles which he had saved and put into a box. The parsimonious habits of his youth were hard to shake off. His master had always taken them to the chandler for the wax to be remoulded.

"Christa, where are the candle stubs I keep in the red box?"

"Ah...I...er...yes..."

"You have moved them? Taken them to Master Chandler perhaps?"

"No... not exactly."

"Then what exactly? You know how costly candles are?"

"Well of course I do. That's why, when I am reading at night before I go to bed, I use up the stubs of the candles, instead of lighting a new one or using one which is still good for you to work by."

"You read by candlelight?"

"I ...er...do."

"You read my books and parchments."

"Well many of them I cannot understand but those which I *do* understand, I *do* read, yes. Into the dark hours."

"Oh...you should be careful, for you will ruin your eyes. My master always said that."

"And I expect he took his own advice, didn't he?"

Bennet laughed out loud. "Hardly ever." He grinned at her. "Oh well. That is a good use of them."

"If you do not want me to use them, then I can stop and save them up."

"No. It's alright. As long as I know that they are being used for the good," he smiled.

Christa had to turn her back to him. She hated to lie to him but how could she tell him that almost every night she was performing a spell which would make him fall in love with her?

All of a sudden, Christa felt guilty. Here she was trying to make this poor man fall for her. It wasn't right. It was unnatural. She vowed to cease her spells straight away.

"I am going to the fleshmongers. Is there anything in particular you want me to buy?"

"Today is St. Gabriel's feast day. Perhaps we should have something special?"

"Ah... you mean your favourite?"

"Lampreys!"

"Lampreys it is, if the good fishman has got them."

He watched her pull on her cloak, tie the woollen ribbons tightly and reach for her basket.

"Your hair is lasting remarkably well."

"Mistress Sempster is good with her hands."

"It is only coming apart just a little *here*." He tucked a stray lock of hair back into the thick plait. His hand brushed her soft cheek and she looked down abruptly. The look sent a frisson through his loins which he had not expected. He turned away.

"I will be working on the chart for Master Poole; perhaps we could work on it together later?"

She smiled and shut the door quickly. A gust of cold wind came in, bringing with it a few autumn leaves, from the tree in Master Weaver's garden.

Christa ploughed through the market. She stopped to catch her breath at the first stall she came to, that of a tinker who was busy mending pots by a little fire.

Her heart was beating madly.

"Cold today," he said.

"Yes, really autumn," she replied, "though you are nice and warm by your fire." She was certainly heated. Her heart was dancing.

"Ach!" the man spat. "The hands are warm, the feet are frozen." He grinned at her with yellow teeth.

"Mistress Christa?"

"Ah...Master Milling."

"How are you?"

"Well, thank you. And you?"

"Better for seeing you."

Now and again this persistent miller had met Christa on the street and much to her dismay had continued to follow her like a lap dog. He was a nice man, it's true, but she just could not feel how he wanted her to feel about him. It was obvious he found her very attractive. She thought him handsome but that was it.

"Is the mill not working today?"

"Ah...we are filling the pond ready for a huge milling of grain. I have a few hours to myself."

"Oh that's good. What will you do with your free time?"

"Walk with you, of course."

She giggled. "Master Milling, I am off to the fleshmongers and then I shall be home straight away. I have much to do at home."

"Then I will accompany you to the shop and home afterwards."

"There is no need," said Christa curtly. "I am perfectly able to do my marketing alone."

"You and that astrologer all alone in that house, what is there to do? What are you going to feed him tonight?"

"Lampreys, if they are available."

"Do you have a good recipe for them?"

"Do you not eat them at your house?"

The man's face became sad. "My mother does very little."

'Ah so,' thought Christa, 'the man lives with his mother.'

"Well good day Master Milling."

"Ben...please."

"Ben," she nodded.

As her head rose from the nod, her eyes looked past him to the side of the road. There by the door of the fleshmonger's, not six yards away from her, stood a figure in a dark cloak. Over her fair hair she wore a dark hood, as working men wear. She stared at Christa.

Christa took in a quick and startled breath.

"Christa? Are you all right?" said Master Milling.

"I have forgotten my purse," said Christa quickly and turned on her heel.

Benedict followed.

"But it is hanging from your belt."

Christa was almost at the door when again she looked back. The woman was still there glaring at her malevolently.

"No money," said Christa fiddling for her new key which Master Lockyer had recently made for her. Her hands shook.

She was suddenly very warm. She felt faint.

She dropped her basket and the world was spinning around her.

Master Benedict Milling caught her as she stumbled against him.

"Christa!"

Just at that moment, Bennet opened the front door.

*****

"Ahem," he said in a sarcastic tone not realising the situation.

"Mistress Christa became unwell. I...don't know why," said Ben.

"Thank you. I have her," said Bennet with poison in his voice.

159

Benedict Milling relinquished the moaning Christa to Bennet's arms and stood back, his hands dangling at his sides.

"I do hope she's all right."

"I will find out what is the matter."

"She just looked towards the fleshmonger's and decided to turn around. She said she had forgotten her money but that wasn't true..."

Bennet narrowed his eyes. He sat Christa down.

"She saw something which made her flee?"

"Well...I don't know. But..."

Bennet rushed to the window and stared out over the road. He could just see the fleshmonger's shop in a gap appearing between a second-hand clothier's and a cobbler's market stall.

There was the figure of a woman in grey.

She stared straight to the window out of which he looked.

He ducked to the side. "Thank you Master...?"

"Milling."

"Thank you."

"I hope the young lady will be alright."

"I am sure she will."

Bennet hurried the man through the door and once he'd locked it, went again to look through the window. The woman had now been joined by a man.

"Well, that was quick. Out with one man, in with another."

He rushed over to Christa who was breathing heavily, her hand on her breast, her eyes closed.

"I saw her...she's here," she said shakily.

"I saw her too."

"Then it was not my imagination?"

"No. She has taken the opportunity to hide in the market crowds."

"She isn't hiding though. She is in full view. Brazen."

"And she's managed to get herself another man."

"Oh, God's blood. She is still angry. Why is she so angry?"

"Come to the window and see if you can see the man," said

Bennet. "You might know him."

Christa slowly approached the window and secretly looked through the bars, hiding herself at the side by the wall.

The man was still there and both of them were now in intimate discussion.

Christa gave a little gulp.

"Oh no!"

"What?"

"You were right when you said that she has found herself another man."

"She is a harpy. She will have inveigled some other poor soul…"

"Ah no, Bennet." Christa pressed herself against him.

Automatically, his arms came around her and she laid her head on his breast.

"You were right. Mistress Ferrers *has* found a new partner. She and my old master are now in league!"

HUNTING THE WREN

CHAPTER TWELVE ~ THE MISTAKE

"How do they know each other?" said Bennet, quickly pulling the locking bar down over the window shutters.

"I would swear they did not know each other when my mistress was alive. When I was at their house."

Bennet sat down and rubbed his chin in thought.

"Ferrers lost her working partner...Kydd."

"Killed him more likely?"

"But why would she? They were running a very successful blackmail business. When things got too rough for them, they'd simply move on to another town. By the charts I cast, they got on very well."

"So if *she* didn't kill him...?"

"Basketwright did."

"But why?"

Bennet closed his eyes and imagined the boorish Basketwright at home after the murder of his wife.

"Would he be taken in too, by the two deceivers, Kydd and Ferrers?"

Christa was tempted to laugh. "No, I don't think so. Though it would not be beyond the realms of possibility that they tried to dupe him in the same way they tried to hoodwink you."

Bennet looked offended. "They didn't succeed."

"And they will not have succeeded with Basketwright either. He is as much a criminal as they are. And just as crafty," said Christa shaking her head.

"So let's imagine that the two of them play out their little lie before him," said Bennet, "As they did here."

"But maybe they failed to hook him...as they failed with you..."

"Er...yes," said Bennet with an embarrassed grin. "And then Basketwright threatens them...maybe follows them and in the ensuing struggle, he kills the man Kydd."

"Now the woman Ferrers is alone and vulnerable. She fears that because she's seen the murder of Kydd, the basket maker will kill her too. And so she strikes a bargain with him?" Christa's face was pale in the relative darkness of the room. "What if she says she will say nothing if Basketwright will go into partnership with her?"

"Of course he will. It is a good and lucrative business and the woman is beautiful...both would appeal to a man like him," said Bennet.

They sat in silence for a while in the semi-darkness of the downstairs room.

"Basketwright did not know where I had gone," said Christa.

"No, but Ferrers knew where you were and she would trade that knowledge for his protection..."

"Such as it is."

"They must be living out at his cottage in Manton."

Bennet peered through the gap in the shutters. The pair had gone.

"It's likely. It's a relatively isolated cottage but near enough to the town. No one will know that they have paired up. Ferrers can continue to extort money from those who have been paying up," he said. "They are unlikely to reveal that they are being blackmailed."

"I wonder who the victims are?" said Christa absently.

"If we knew that then we might have some information to go on. We could approach them and..."

"You think they'd own up?"

"Maybe not."

"What can we do?"

"We need to find some evidence which links the two, Ferrers and Basketwright. And if we could, finding some evidence of the money they've extorted from people would be good."

"How on earth can we do that?" said Christa almost laughing. "Unless we..."

Bennet looked up at her, his face glowing.

"Oh no...Bennet!" she cried. "No!"

"We can't live our lives locked up in the house in constant fear," said Bennet angrily. "We have to face them."

"But they are killers, both of them. How can we do that? You are thinking of going to the house, aren't you?"

Bennet ranged around the room as a condemned man might pace about his cell.

"We have to find some evidence which links them together and to the murder of Kydd."

"No, Bennet, please. He will kill you."

"It must be accomplished when he...they are out of the house. Then I'll go and search."

He stopped in the middle of the room. "Saturday...will he be out with his wares at the market?"

"He isn't there today and does he need to sell baskets if he has found a much easier and more lucrative job?" said Christa.

"Perhaps I can ask Harry to help?"

"No...you mustn't. He is one of the people who helps the town reeve. He is bound to tell the authorities that you are planning on house breaking. He must."

Bennet wasn't listening to her.

"I need to go and watch the house for a while, see what their routines are. See if they are indeed there together."

"Oh Bennet please...don't go."

At last he listened to her and his gaze took in her worried face.

"Don't worry, I won't get caught."

"You can't know that."

"I... have a way of knowing...things," he said mysteriously.

"You would cast a chart for..."

"It has already been done."

"What?"

Bennet licked his lips and grabbed her arm, "Come with me a moment."

In the upper room, Bennet reached under his mattress and brought out the black book.

"You remember I told you a while ago that my master had plotted my next few months...that he was incredibly accurate about what was going on in my life?"

"You did say something..."

"After he died, he left me this book. In it he has written something almost every day. Last night I read a piece which told me that I was searching for something. He has mentioned this a few times over the past few months. He said that I was searching and would find out something I needed."

"Something? But will you be safe? Does it say you'll be safe?"

"He said that there would be some danger but that the wren would aid me as she always did."

Christa's nose wrinkled, "The wren? A little brown bird?"

"Ah no...I think..." Bennet stopped talking in the middle of a sentence. Did he dare reveal that Christa was present in the book and that his master had predicted her arrival and referred to her as The Wren?

"I think he was talking about...you...Christa."

"Me? But why should I...?"

They both jumped from their skins as there was a harsh banging on the door.

"Astrologer...come out here?"

"Oh Jesus...it's him!" cried Christa, crossing herself.

Bennet gritted his teeth and reached for his quarterstaff.

"Then the meeting is to be earlier than we thought."

Bennet threw back the bolt and quickly opened the door. He could see several people out in the roadway.

"Mistress Alleyn? How nice to see you." Bennet laid the quarterstaff of which he'd had a firm hold, by the door and smiled.

"We'll not come in..." said an angry voice.

Bennet peered around the few faces he knew.

One angry man stepped forward.

"You don't know me. And no, it's not nice to see you but it is good to put a name to your poxed face, Master Astrologer."

The man's face contorted in anger. "Bennet Celest, liar and cheat."

"I beg your pardon?"

"Liar... and cheat."

"Mistress Alleyn, can you...?" Bennet looked towards the woman and to his dismay saw that she had been crying. Crying for a very long time and was in deep distress.

"This is my husband, Master Celest. Listen to him," she sobbed.

Other people passing by were now interested in the scene unfolding before the astrologer's door. They craned their necks and stood on tiptoe to get a glimpse of this monster. This so called cheat and liar.

"You told my wife that she had to take our daughter Alys away... our little pride and joy just two years old . Away from a contagion in the town."

"Yes... I did. I admit it. She was in great danger if she stayed."

"She didn't stay. Margaret took her to Ramsbury."

Bennet's stomach lurched and he felt nauseous. Surely he had not been wrong.

"Well, Master Astrologer...you were right. She was in great danger. Such danger that...", the man swallowed and put his shaking hand to his forehead, "our little angel died. You told us that if she was removed from the town she would be safe. You lied. Master Celest!"

"Alys is dead…?"

"She died, they say, of an asphyxiation of her lungs. You're a liar and you cheat people of their money."

"Yes, she was always vulnerable to…That's why I…"

"She died and you said that if we took her away she would be safe."

"I truly thought that she *would* be safe."

"Liar!"

"Is there contagion in Ramsbury town?" said Bennet, red faced and beginning to sweat.

"We moved her from a safe place, her home here in the town, to a place of death and destruction, upon *your* advice. And now she's dead."

Mistress Alleyn turned to a neighbour and wept into her breast. The woman spat at Bennet.

More folk joined in the insults.

"I can assure you that the work I did on Alys' chart indicated that she would be safe removed from this town to another place. I wasn't to know that there was also contagion in Ramsbury," shouted Bennet over the throng.

"No one here has had it…you liar," said one man, "Marlbury is safe."

"I can assure you Master Hettler, there will be illness in the town. If it is not here yet. I*t will come!*"

"Pah!" People started to throw things.

"Liar"

"Incompetent!"

"Murderer!"

One man came into the door hole and threw a punch at Bennet. He didn't see it coming and took the blow full on the face, reeling backwards. But the man did not follow with any further violence.

Bennet's last appeal of, "I am sorry if I did not see the whole truth of it but it will come!" disappeared into a barrage of dung and mud and mouldy cabbage leaves left behind from the market.

The astrologer leapt up and slammed and bolted the door.

The heckling went on for quite some time and some folk went to the shutters to try and break them by throwing stones. They held firm.

Christa sat trembling in the corner. "Little Alys Alleyn?" she asked "I saw her chart."

Bennet was dumbfounded.

"I cast her chart and progressed it." He stared wildly into space. "It said that she was in danger of a congestion to the chest. It would be as a result of some contagion she would contract here in Marlborough town."

"But her mother took her away on your advice *into* the contagion not away from it?"

Bennet sat and put his head in his hands. "My master said I would make a mistake. He said that I would live with this for the rest of my life. The death of little Alys."

Christa came up to him and took his head into her hands, cradling it to her bosom.

"You did what you thought was right. Hush now, you were not to know."

Bennet sniffled "My master told me. He said 'We may only see what we are allowed to see. We may not influence what is there, only reflect the truth of it. What will be...will be."

Christa went down on her knees before him and took his hands.

"You were trying to save a small child. You did something wrong but for all the right reasons, it seems. Let me tend to your hurt."

"We cannot change what is to be. We can try but we cannot change it," he said. Christa felt like joining him in his weeping.

"You are only a man, Bennet. You care about people. You were only trying to help.

In time they will come to realise you were right and were only trying to aid them."

Bennet rubbed his nose with the back of his hand "They will!" he said forcefully, "When the contagion comes to Marlborough and people start to drop with it. Then they will see I was right. It is here. Perhaps it was too late for little Alys and she already had it when she was taken to Ramsbury."

"You really think there will be a terrible illness which will kill people in the town?"

"I do. And it is coming soon. I am surprised it is not showing here already."

*****

Bennet *was* right,

The fever, lung congestion, pain in the limbs and joints and sore throat came within the week.

Of course the first person it took hold of was Mistress Alleyn.

She was young and fit and did not die but she gave it to her mother and she *did* die.

The Saturday market went on as normal and Bennet did not go looking for the basket maker and his doxy. He stayed at home brooding upon the death of little Alys. No one came to visit him. No one engaged him to work for them. Word had travelled about the town as quickly as the contagion. Weeks went by and Bennet had to draw on his savings to keep Christa and himself afloat. Luckily he had much coin stored with the Jews and was not too worried. As Christa had said, "The town will have a short memory. They will be back once they have forgotten. And forget they will."

It was Harry, weeks later, who brought them the news that the contagion seemed to have done its worst and that the little town was recovering both in health and in its capacity to forget.

"My master. Gilbert Cordwainer and I have done our level best to spread the word that you predicted this terrible episode. That you warned the town. Quite apart from saying that the young and old would die, which of course you did, you got it right when you said that it would come soon. The fact it perhaps came from Ramsbury to the town and not from the town to elsewhere is neither here or there. Folk are beginning to see that you were not wrong...well...not very wrong anyway."

"I was not wrong."

"No."

"But I was wrong in trying to change the course of things."

"How?"

"I should not have interfered. I should have let nature take its course. Little Alys would die anyway. She always *would* die. God wanted to take her. I could not prevent it."

Bennet sighed and aimlessly wandered around the upper room.

Christa looked despairingly at Harry.

"He will work again?" she whispered.

Harry put his hand on Christa's shoulder, "I am sure of it."

"So who has died Harry?" said Bennet. "Anyone we know?"

"Those who live on the Marsh and at the bottom of Figgins Lane seem to have taken the brunt of it."

"Aye well. The poorest folk live there. The houses are unsanitary and the night vapours from the river are unwholesome. It's no surprise. They have poor health anyway."

"Master Turner is dead as is his wife."

"Oh I am sorry about that."

"The senior Hettlers have succumbed."

"Ah... they are related to Mistress Alleyn, God rest them."

"And your Master Benedict Milling has been very ill but he managed to shake it off. He's young and strong."

"He's not my Master Milling!" said Christa in exasperation.

"You were right when you said it would be the young and the old. His old mother died of it."

"Oh!" said Christa sadly.

"The Old Goldsmith..." added Harry.

"Ah... the grandfather?"

"Aye Master Metier senior. And the cheeseman, senior."

"Ah well...his liver was always…"

"And Mistress Sempster across the way."

"No!" said Christa, jumping up. "She can't be dead."

"I am afraid she is, as is her near neighbour, Mistress Kitchener."

"You knew her didn't you Christa?" said Bennet. "She was kind to you."

"Aye she was very kind. I made her a bag pudding…" she trailed off with a lump in her throat which seemed as if she had swallowed the whole of one of her bag puddings.

"Ah well. Many will remember that you said it was coming. So I think that you'll soon see a queue forming outside your door again," said Harry with a smile.

Bennet nodded half-heartedly. He had almost given in. The death of Alys had made him concerned for the calling he followed. He was close to believing that it was all unworthy and that he would never again cast a chart. His confidence was shattered.

"Have you heard anything of Basketwright...or that woman Ferrers, Harry?"

"Not recently. Why, is she bothering you again?"

Christa told him about the episode a few weeks ago at the market. "We think that they have joined forces."

"God's Almighty Christians!" said Harry aghast. "The two of them together?"

"We think that they murdered Kydd and have set up their business...again though with the contagion things have slowed down a little. Perhaps they have not been able to work their deceit. Perhaps they've moved to another town."

"If we never see them again…"

"Can we hope the contagion has taken them?" said Harry with a rueful smile.

But no. That was not to be.

*****

The night grew very dark.

Bennet had decided that he would go to the cottage in Manton again just to see if the felons were actually there together. Christa desperately tried to dissuade him.

"You stay here and I'll be back as soon as I can," he said.

Christa felt agitated, "No...don't go Bennet. They will find you and kill you. They'll know you're there."

"I just want to look for some evidence that they are both at the house, that's all. Then I can tell the town reeve."

"Then I am not staying here. I will come with you."

"No...no...that makes things doubly dangerous."

"I can't let you go on your own," whined Christa on the edge of tears.

"I am your master and I say you stay *here.*"

Before she could argue further, he slipped out of the door into the night.

Christa waited a little while and then, keeping to the darkness of buildings, tree and hedge, she followed.

She hadn't realised how difficult it was to track someone in the pitch black. Nor how hard it was to keep on one's path when it wasn't possible to see the usual landmarks visible by day. She stumbled into bushes and tripped over stones several times but somehow righted herself and always knew that Bennet was just ahead of her on the river path.

The river to her right, trickled onward, an almost silent silver band save for the odd night animal rustling in the plants to the bank and the occasional plop in the water.

She stopped to get her bearings. It was a straight road to Manton. Past the castle mill, onward past St. George's Preshute and then a bend to the big barn.

Here she waited until she could locate the house where she had lived many years, as servant to the basket makers.

Christa had imagined that everything would be silent around the house but it was not. Quiet voices came from the ground floor of the ill lit house.

She peered round the outhouse where the rushes and willows were stored. The door was always open and she ducked in quickly feeling less vulnerable with walls around her and a roof over her head.

Bennet was somewhere out there in the courtyard. She had to fight off the terrible urge to go and search for him. She knew it wasn't wise and that any distraction would be dangerous for them both. If Bennet was discovered, she had to remain unseen in order to be able to get help, if she was able.

She ducked from the door again and out into the courtyard. It seemed to her that her footsteps sounded loud on the packed earth but truly they were loud only to her ears.

The little tawny owls which nested in the old tree at the back of the dairy building, gave out their autumn alarm call. They were not hooting their major call often now for the mating season and the guarding of territory was over. But they still screeched when surprised. It made Christa jump and she crossed herself. Owls were the birds of evil.

She listened carefully. She made out two voices speaking far off. One of them was definitely her old master. She would know his belligerent tone anywhere.

He was on the edge of anger. She heard him say,

"So you'll let every Tom, Dick or Harry tup you, but not me?"

A quiet controlled voice answered. It was not easy to tell what was said but, "That's work. They never get...I don't want..." It was the woman Ferrers.

So they *were* here together. Surely Bennet, wherever he was, could hear that the two of them were in collusion. Surely now he would turn and make for home. And safety.

"Aw c'mon. You've not been so modest in the past. Let me just..."

said Basketwright.

"No. I told you. Not tonight."

"And it wasn't last night either. Nor the night before that."

There was a sharp sound like something being thrown. "Jesus, when will I get a chance to...You know you'll give in if I beat you..."

"Threats will get you nowhere."

So the two felons were not happy together. They were arguing. What a surprise?

Christa pressed her cheek to the wall.

"You're as bad as my missus. Always saying no."

'Ah, thought Christa, I have heard this conversation before.' The woman was denying the man sexual favours. Yes, her mistress had tried that one but it usually ended badly and she'd had to capitulate.

Tears welled up in Christa's eyes as she recalled all the times she'd heard such arguments between the basket workers. And the times poor Margaret hadn't won.

She'd had to listen to her sobbing as the man had his way with her and to his contented snoring afterwards. Once she had crawled out of her little room and gone to her mistress to offer her solace. The drunken Basketwright had woken and beat her with a withy rod. Her mistress had just looked on, terrified of the man. Christa never entered the room again at night when they were sleeping.

Now there was silence. Christa stretched her ears.

"I said get off!"

There was a slap and a shuffling sound and Christa recognised the growl of Basketwright as he became more incensed and lustful.

"Hit me would you, you trull!" There was a prolonged scuffle.

The woman cried out "Ow!"

Christa then heard, "Now! You'll do as you're told." She heard the woman breathing hard.

After a while she heard, "Come on then...come on, you bully," This was the voice of the woman Ferrers. "Not so happy now I have a knife are you?"

Christa could tell by the voices, that there was now some space between them.

"Come any closer and I'll cut the bloody thing off."

Rage took hold of the man and he screeched an inarticulate cry which made Christa jump.

Had she stuck him? No. He was still speaking

"How difficult must it be to let me...?" The man was trying his best to cajole. "Come on... I only want a little peek."

"Stay away."

"A little feel of your bubbies then?"

"I said no!"

"Aw, Jehanne, you know I'll get my way. One way or another. And it's best for you one way and not the other."

"One more step and I'll stick you, God help me, I will. How did I ever think this was a good idea, after Gerard was killed? I would..." Christa missed the last words in a sound which she thought denoted that the basket maker had rushed the woman.

There was a scuffle with muted voices and heavy breathing and grunting sounds which Christa thought was the two of them struggling.

Then there was an exasperated scream cut off quickly, perhaps by a hand to the mouth. The struggling continued and then there was a rush of air expelled.

"Ah!" a wounded cry? A man.

Christa stretched her ears but there was silence.

Then after a while came a pained grunt. A shuffle of feet. An oath - "God's blood."

It was the basket weaver.

Once again it seemed as if furniture and items were being thrown around. The outer door opened violently and a figure staggered out falling flat as it met the night air. There was no doubt the man was drunk.

"Jesus!" he said.

The basket maker picked himself up, staggered a little more and made for the river a hundred yards away. Christa tried to listen for a splash but there was nothing.

She scurried from her hiding place and called quietly.

"Bennet." It was almost a whisper.

No answer.

Looking back over her shoulder in case the basket man should return, Christa ran to the main door of the house. At the same time Bennet came round the end of the house wall.

"Jesus, Christa, you gave me a fright."

Christa was breathing hard even though she had not exerted herself. "He'll be back...we must go." She grabbed his sleeve.

But Bennet was already peering into the house.

"I told you to stay at home..."

"Well I didn't do as I was told."

Bennet straightened for he had been trying to make himself as small as possible in his passage round the buildings.

"Did you hear them?" said Christa.

"Of course I did, it would be impossible *not* to hear them."

Bennet's eyes raked the interior of the cottage. "Oh God!" He plunged into the house.

"Bennet!"

She could see him bending over something on the floor.

"Bennet! We should go now. This isn't good."

"No it isn't," she heard him say as she saw him go down on one knee and reach out.

Again she peered into the gloom out by the river. She could see and hear nothing. At least the basket maker was not returning immediately. But they needed to be gone when he did.

"Bennet! Now! We need to go before the man comes back."

"I doubt he'll be back, Christa."

"What?"

His pained face strained up to her by the light of two tallow candles.

"He's killed her."

"What?"

"Basketwright has killed Ferrers. She's dead." He lifted his bloodied hand to her sight.

At that very moment, they both heard the tread of heavy feet and a man came round the corner of the dairy building, making directly for them. In his hand he gripped a quarterstaff.

"Ha! I might have known it was you."

Bennet got up from the floor and faced the man who was standing in the doorway.

"Jonas Pike! What are you here for?"

The man hefted his quarterstaff aggressively.

"Me? I have a right to be here. I'm on the night watch for master reeve. What are you...doing...?" His gaze went past the astrologer and lit upon the body of Ferrers lying on the beaten earth floor.

"Well...at last, I have you...*Master Astrologer!*"

"What...? I found her dead."

"That man Basketwright killed her. We heard it happen," said Christa quickly.

Pike leaned over the dead woman.

"Oh yeah? Then why are *you* covered in her blood?"

"Her wound was still spilling when I went to her aid, just before she died. Of course I am bloodied."

"I didn't see anyone else," said Pike, his eyes glittering.

"Then you weren't watching very well were you?" said Christa nastily. "Or listening!"

Pike gave her a withering look and then marched up to Bennet. "Red handed. You always wanted to get even didn't you...? First the man, now the woman."

"Now wait a moment..." began Christa but Pike pushed her away. "You can hold your tongue you strutting slut!"

"I beg your pardon."

"I said shut it!"

He grabbed Bennet by the arm. "C'mon then *Master Astrologer.* I'm taking you in for murder."

"He didn't murder her, you stinky fish head!" yelled Christa in anger.

Pike turned on her and before she could move, he'd struck her full in the face. She reeled backwards; he'd split her lip.

Bennet tried to retaliate but Pike grabbed him round the neck and squeezed, pushing him up against the wall of the cottage.

"You come quietly or I'll give her more of where that came from." He nodded at Christa.

"Leave it be, Bennet," said Christa holding her mouth as the blood flowed.

"Right, now, you march over to that small hut there and we'll just make you secure."

Bennet turned and trudged in front of the reeve's man.

He hadn't gone five paces when he suddenly spun round and struck Pike in the midriff.

But Pike's muscles were as hard as a sorcerer's heart. He was, after all, a blacksmith by trade. He merely smiled nastily and gave Bennet a buffet on the head with his quarterstaff. Bennet fell heavily to the ground, out cold.

Christa screamed.

But before she did, and before Bennet had drawn back his arm to hit the man Pike, she had seen him grimace, his eyes swivel to the road as if to say, "Run, Christa, run."

And so she ran.

CHAPTER THIRTEEN
THE MASTER'S WORDS

Pike was too busy lifting Bennet up in order to get him into the shed, to chase Christa. She ran off in the direction of the river but then thought better of it and veered off into the fields surrounding the tiny village. She had no wish to meet the despicable Basketwright on his return journey. If indeed he would come back to their cottage.

She ran on blindly through the fields and picked up the road to the town at the other side of Preshute. Her breath came in short bursts and she began to get a stitch in her side. She was far enough away now and she slowed down. She had ricked her ankle on stones, caught her clothes on brambles and scratched herself on twigs and her swollen lip throbbed in rhythm with her heart beats.

She was worried. Very worried about Bennet. Where could she go to get help? She thought about going to the town reeve to tell him what had happened but somehow she didn't trust the authorities.

She reached the outskirts of the town. Panic set in. Where should she go? Could she go home? Who could she tell? She crossed the bridge and looked up at the stars, 'Oh, stars...planets...tell me what I should do?'

She walked on; the town was silent and the stars did not answer her.

But, passing the cordwainer's shop, she looked up at the face of the building. She knew that all the main living quarters were at the back of the shop; the parlour was on the first floor, the top floor housed the two apprentices. They slept in the one roomed attic.

Reaching for some small stones from the road she lobbed them up at the shutters on the window, set just below the roof.

She threw several times before the shutter opened gingerly.

"Harry," she hissed. "Harry come down please...it's really important."

"Jesus, Christa...do you know what hour of night it is?"

"Please Harry. It's Bennet; he's in trouble.

*****

Harry drew her into the darkness of the gate to the priory immediately next door to the cordwainer's property.

"Harry..." Christa leaned into him tiredly. "What am I to do?"

"You say that he has been taken up by that man Pike for the murder of the woman Ferrers?"

"She was there with my old master, I told you. We heard them arguing and then the basket weaver struck her with a knife and abruptly left the house..."

"Where is the basket weaver now?"

"I have no idea. But Bennet has been locked in an outhouse. That man Pike will come back with the town reeve in the morning and Bennet will be taken up for the murder of Ferrers. But he didn't kill her. He can't have killed her. He was standing outside the house with me at the time."

Harry Glazer rubbed his chin. "You are absolutely certain it was the basket maker?"

"Yes. And I am not sure if the woman did not manage to wound him before he turned her own knife on her and killed her."

"He's wounded?"

"Possibly. I heard him cry out and swear. And when he left...I saw

182

him. He seemed uncertain. Sluggish. But then, he was drunk."

Harry ran his hands through his hair. "If the town reeve finds out I have been helping a suspected felon…"

"Harry, he's not guilty. He's not guilty of anything, except caring too much and wanting to put things right."

"He's a fool to go out there and tackle them."

"I told him so," said Christa, "but he wouldn't listen. He ordered me to stay away but I couldn't leave him. Oh Harry, I love him. I can't let anything awful happen to him. Please…help him."

She fell against him then, weeping, touching his breast.

He lifted her chin. "And Pike struck you too?"

She nodded.

He patted her back. "Then let's return and see if we can somehow get Bennet out."

"Oh Harry thank you… thank you."

"He is my best friend, you understand that, but I will not break the law for him, do you comprehend Christa? We can get him away from that odious man Pike but we must tell the truth to Master Barbflet."

"No…no…"

Harry turned her round. "Come let's get to the hut and back before it gets light."

"If we get him out…where can we go? You know they are sure to look in our house."

"Never mind that. I have a plan. I was once in terrible trouble and accused of murder…I know what to do."

"You? Murder?" she said with a little uncertainty.

"Yes…but I was cleared. I will tell you about it as we walk."

He took her small hand in his and together they ran back along the road to Manton.

The place was silent and the candles which had lit the cottage had guttered out.

"Where is Pike holding him?" whispered Harry.

"Here." Christa leaned against the door of the small wooden store.

"Bennet... Bennet..." she hissed. "Oh no. He managed to strike Bennet on the head. I hope he hasn't killed him."

"Pike struck him too?"

"Yes. With his quarterstaff to subdue him."

"Jesus!" Harry licked his lips. "Bennet... Bennet are you in there?" He tried the door.

"Look...there's only a bar across. It has no lock. My old master kept his small handcart here. He hardly ever uses it now he has the big one," said Christa.

Harry lifted the bar and tossed it away. Silently they listened for any movement. There was no one else about.

Throwing open the door, Harry saw Bennet was lying on his back on the beaten earth, his forehead glistening with blood.

"Oh no..." Christa went down on her knees and lovingly raised Bennet's head.

"Bennet..." She noticed that most of the blood had dried and that there was very little new flow.

Bennet groaned.

Harry gave the cart a cursory search. "It seems safe enough."

He lifted the astrologer up by the knees and shoulders and placed him gently on the bed of the empty handcart.

"I'll get the cart out of the shed, Christa. God has given us a tool. It would be churlish not to use it."

Christa found some sacks and wrapped Bennet in them. If they met anyone, they would not readily see what burden they carried.

She said as much to Harry who was manhandling the cart through the small door.

"We are not likely to meet anyone just yet. It's a little past the third hour of prayer. Sunrise is not until the first hour after lauds at this time of year."

And most folk go to matins...later in the morning," added Christa.

"Yes, you're right. Come - we wheel. Take hold of a bar and pull."

*****

As they ran the little handcart along the road, Harry told Christa the story of his brush with the law.

"I was accused of murdering my father."

"Goodness, your *father?*"

"Yes. He was a beast of a man and makes this Basketwright look like a saint."

Christa guffawed. She couldn't imagine anyone worse than Basketwright.

"He preyed on girls...please don't say anything to anyone. It's a secret. Bennet knows and a few other folk but it's not general knowledge. It would reflect badly on me you see, if it were known that..."

"I promise. How did you escape?"

"I ran into sanctuary at Durley where the county Constable lives. He's a friend of my master's, Gilbert Cordwainer, and together they secured my innocence and found the real culprit."

They were now approaching the town bridge and Bennet was beginning to come round in the back of the cart.

"Ooooh...my head feels like it's ..." Bennet sat up and looked around. "Harry... Harry... that you?"

"It is my good friend. Do you think you might walk? I'd like to leave this cart away from the town if I can. Then no one knows exactly where in Marlborough we have gone. For now at any rate."

Bennet clambered down unsteadily with a great deal of help. Christa held him up and grasped him around the waist. He looked down and smiled at her as best he could.

"Where are we going?"

"The other end of town," said Harry, pushing the cart into the bushes. "Now we walk. If we see anyone, we must hide."

But they saw no one in their long, arduous struggle up the High Street.

Bennet's legs would not obey him and now and again he staggered. Christa, though much smaller and less strong than Harry, took most of his weight upon herself. A fact that was not lost upon Harry.

Eventually they reached the dark maw of the alleyway to the church of St. Mary.

Christa baulked at the door. "The church? How is that a safe haven?"

"Sanctuary. Bennet will be safe here for forty days and forty nights…" He pushed open the door, "And we then have a chance to clear his name."

"But…"

"Trust me, Christa. It's a place of safety."

"What if Basketwright is still alive and he gets wind of where Bennet is? He'll have no compunction about coming in and disposing of him, even if it is a church. He is a Godless man."

Harry gnawed at his lip.

"I think Master Barbflet will post a guard at the door to prevent Bennet from escaping."

"Oh!"

"It is the standard practice. I think Basketwright will have difficulty passing *them*."

They struggled to the frith chair with a semi-conscious Bennet between them and sat him down. His head nodded on his chest.

"We need to get the doctor. We don't know what damage has been done to Bennet's head…" said Christa. "He's obviously not right."

Again Harry gnawed his lip. "You go. Explain everything to him. He's a good man." Luckily the doctor's house was close by the church.

When she was gone, Harry raced from the church to the small cottage close by where lived Father Torold, the priest of St. Mary's.

"A sanctuary seeker?" said the priest, shrugging on his dark robes. "Well! I haven't had one of those since…let me think, it must have been somewhere around 1199…"

"Hurry please father."

Once the words had been spoken by the priest the sanctuary seeker could not legally be removed from his place of safety, not even by the sheriff's authorities. It was the law.

Father Torold was finishing his speech when the doctor arrived. "And you will abjure the realm..."

"No! No. I will not...I have done nothing," said Bennet groggily.

"Torold...leave it for the moment," said Doctor Johannes, "He's in no fit state to understand what is being said."

The priest shrugged. "Nevertheless I must say it."

Bennet was very anxious, tossing about on the frith stool.

Christa's voice echoed in the high vault of the nave. "Master Bennet Celest, do as you are told for once. Let those who are willing to help you, help you."

Harry, the priest and the doctor exchanged wry glances.

Bennet slumped on the stool.

The doctor went to work on his head.

Harry looked up at the east window. "It's a little before dawn. Should I go down to the town reeve and report the night's events?"

"Go," said Torold, "he will make contact with the coroner. He too needs to be involved."

Harry laid a comforting hand on Christa's arm. "I will be back as soon as I can."

Christa backed off to allow the men to minister to Bennet and went into the nave, to the steps which led to the chancel of the church. Kneeling there, she prayed; prayed that Bennet would be believed and that all would work in their favour, though a little niggle at the back of her brain would not let her rest.

"Where has Basketwright gone?" she muttered. "As long as he is alive, we are in danger."

She prayed some more. Prayed as she had never before done in her life.

*****

The town reeve looked sternly under his eyebrows.

"So, if I understand this correctly, you both went to check to see if the man Basketwright had gone back to his home?"

"Yes...he was there with that woman Ferrers," said Christa

"And we heard the quarrel between them."

"A quarrel which ended in her being stabbed?"

"Yes."

"But you didn't actually see it because you were outside the door?"

"We heard every word. Both of us."

"Why do we have to go over and over it? We've told you what happened," said Bennet, exasperation and exhaustion in his voice.

"I like to get to the heart of a person's recollection. And if it means asking over and over then...."

"What you mean is, you ask over and over in order to trip someone up," said Christa with a jut of her chin. "When they make a mistake."

Barbflet gave a loud exhalation. "So where is the man now?"

"I don't know. We don't know. He ran off in the direction of the river."

"Your man was there, Jonas Pike. He was on duty tonight, patrolling the cottage. He would know perhaps where the man went. After he locked me in the shed, he..."

"Pike was there?"

"We told you, he gave Bennet a buffet on the head and he struck me...see..." Christa turned her head to the light now coming through the east window.

She had a fairly large pink and blue bruise on her cheekbone and a split lip.

Barbflet looked strangely at Harry. "Pike? Did you see him there?"

"No, sir, I ..."

"What were you doing with these two anyway, Glazer?"

"Ah...I ...err..."

"I asked him to help," said Christa confidently. "It's my fault."

"I arrived...after the...erm...incident, sir."

Barbflet groaned. "God's teeth, this gets more and more tangled. I will have to explain all this to the Constable."

"Yes sir."

Barbflet sat on the chancel steps. "What was Pike doing there?" The red sanctuary light made his face glow.

"You hadn't asked him to take the watch?" asked Harry.

"Why would I do that? We had no reason to believe that the basket man was still in the town. We were no longer watching his house."

"Then Pike was there for some reason of his own."

Barbflet looked worried. "When it gets fully light, I'll send a party out to find Pike. Meanwhile, I am afraid I will have to put you, Bennet, in the lockup."

"Ah..." Father Torold intervened. "I have offered him the sanctuary of St. Mary's. He cannot be removed from the church, Master Barbflet."

Barbflet looked puzzled. "Bennet. Do you know what's at stake? If you take sanctuary?"

"Sir?"

"You must admit your guilt, whether or not you *are* guilty. You have two choices then, after forty days. Give yourself over to the law as a self-confessed guilty man and be tried or abjure the realm... leave these shores forever, never to return."

"I am *not* guilty."

"Then why admit it?"

Bennet looked around the people crowded around the frith chair.

"And if I go into captivity?"

"You will be held at the castle gaol until the justices arrive and they will hear your case."

"That might be months," said Harry with a worried expression. "You may not survive to be tried, Bennet."

"Sir, please believe me, I didn't do it."

Barbflet stared at Bennet for a long while. "I am inclined to believe you Master Celest but I have not the authority…"

"Sir… do you believe in the power of the stars? Of the planets?" said Bennet standing up shakily.

"I…um…do I *believe*? Well, I think the answer must be yes to that. How can I not?"

Doctor Johannes, present at the back of the group, cleared his throat.

"Oh I know, Johannes, that you are somewhat sceptical…but the rest of us mere mortals…"

"Then let me show you something which may prove my innocence," said Bennet.

"I beg your pardon?"

Bennet closed his eyes against the terrible headache now surging through his temples and thought.

He would use his book. His little black book. Surely if they read what his master had written they would see that he was innocent of any crime.

"I have a book. At home."

"No, Bennet!" said Christa, worried that this would undermine his case.

"It is a book which was written by my old master."

"Geoffrey?"

"He plotted the course of my life from the day he died to…I am not sure when it ceases for I was forbidden by him to look at any other page but the one which has the day's date on it."

"It has been incredibly accurate, "said Christa, though truly she wasn't really sure what information the book contained, save that she was mentioned in it and was referred to as the wren.

"I can tell you where it is and you may read it."

The town reeve and the priest looked at each other in amazement.

"Go and fetch it. Read it. It should tell you what is happening to me and why. It will, I am sure, explain that I am entirely innocent of any wrongdoing."

"You would allow us to read something you say you have not read yourself?"

"I will."

"Then you have great faith in your dead master, Geoffrey."

"I do."

"Wait…" said Johannes the doctor. "How do we know this book was definitely written by Geoffrey? Could you not have written it yourself?"

"You, of all men, Master Doctor, will know the hand of Geoffrey Celest. You saw his work more often than many people. You, I am sure will verify it."

There was a silence in the church and sounds from outside now began to filter in. The tramp of folk coming to church for Matins.

"Oh, I must ring the bell!" said the good father as he disappeared to his ringing room.

"I don't think it's a good idea for you to be seen here Bennet," said the town reeve quickly. "Come we shall go back to your house and recover this book. If, as you say it allows for any doubt about your guilt, you may go free. If not, then I must either return you to sanctuary or take you to the castle."

Christa gave a huge sigh. She had not quite the faith in the book which Bennet had, but she hoped against hope that Bennet's dead master's words would prove his blamelessness.

She crossed herself before the altar again and gave a quick prayer before following the town reeve, Harry, Bennet and the doctor out of the church by the west door just as folk were coming in at the south.

*****

They crowded into the top room at Bennet's house.

Bennet removed the book from its hiding place and gave it into the hands of the town reeve.

Nicholas Barbflet was an educated man; he was able to read the easy Latin well.

He purposefully sat down on the stool by the window.

"Here sir is the letter my master wrote to me before he died. He predicted the day, indeed the hour of his death to the last ray of the sun…"

Johannes of Salerno took the parchment and scanned it.

'This will come as a surprise to you, dear Bennet. My dear Bennet. You are the best, the very best of men and the most able student I have ever taught and I grieve to say what I must say and at the same time rejoice that it is to you, I entrust my whole enterprise, built up over forty years.'

He looked up. "This is indeed his hand." He read aloud.

"'I have been an astrologer for over forty years. I have not restricted myself to the great and the good, for as far as I am concerned, the little people are as much in need of our help as the great.' "This certainly sounds like the man Geoffrey whom I knew," said Johannes. "'I might have made a huge amount of money had I confined my work to the doings of those who could pay great amounts for my knowledge. But I did not. And I know that you will be as am I, drawn to those little folk, for forgive me, Bennet I have cast your natal horoscope and I know you intimately from its findings.'"

Johannes scanned the rest quickly with a mumbling under his breath.

"He goes on to say that he will leave the world this year 1207, upon the fourth day of July at about vespers. He says his heart will give out. He leaves everything to Bennet."

Bennet added from memory, "'It has been a pleasure and an honour to teach you, Bennet and I know that you will carry on my good work. God bless you and keep you.

Until we meet again.

Geoffrey.'

Johannes nodded. "That is what it says."

Barbflet scanned the first page of the black book.

"The fourth day of July 1207 -'Upon the day of my death which is the first day of your life as a master astrologer - you will suffer an attempt to relieve you of your purse but it will fail.'

Barbflet looked up. Bennet nodded.

"I was in the church porch when it happened. If you ask Master Vyvyan Fuller, he will tell you that I spoke to him about the incident shortly afterwards."

Barbflet read on. "You will have difficulty getting my body from this upper room. The window is the obvious choice but the stairs will be chosen and you will drop my corpse. For which I do forgive you." Barbflet's lip twitched in humour.

"If you ask the two men who collect the corpses for St. Mary's, they will tell you this too is the truth."

"You are certain this is the hand of our friend Master Celest... Geoffrey Celest?" said the town reeve.

The doctor nodded. "It *is* his writing."

Barbflet went on turning the pages. The meeting with Christa and Mistress Basketwright was there. The warning of the danger the basket maker's wife was in. The temptation by Ferrers and the man Kydd. The death of little Alys.

Barbflet made sure he read every day. It took some time.

Christa watched Bennet's face as his life was laid bare in detail.

"There are pages which are blank. Just the day...?"

"My master felt that there was nothing particularly worthy to write about on those days. They are the days of the pestilence." The town reeve grunted.

And then they came to the present day.

"I have not read this day, sir," said Bennet "What you read there is as new to me as it is to you."

Christa held her breath.

"You will be reading this aloud. Master Barbflet and Bennet will have no knowledge of what I write, for he will not have been able to read this. He has been in some danger, which is not yet past. The young wren too, is in danger. Bennet is guiltless of any error, save that of being over fond of his fellow man and poking his nose in where he feels he can be of help."

"Jesus!" said Harry. "He was an amazing astrologer wasn't he?"

Bennet nodded, tears in his eyes. "He was."

Master Barbflet turned the next page.

"Please sir, do not read it to me. I am forbidden to know the words my master wrote for tomorrow."

Barbflet turned from the assembly and mouthed the words to himself. He nodded, closed the book and gave it back to Bennet.

"You are absolved of all guilt, Bennet. I will write a report to that effect." He took hold of the doctor's arm, who was looking a little shocked and confused.

"Come Johannes, let's leave the pair."

He turned at the stair head. "Bennet Celest stay out of trouble. Do your job. Leave the law to us. I do not want to be fishing *your* corpse out of the river one morning!"

Bennet nodded shamefacedly.

"Ah... Mistress Christa..." Johannes leaned forward and put a little pot onto the table. "Salve for your bruises."

"Thank you sir."

*****

Harry, Christa and Bennet were now alone.

Harry was still amazed at the predictions which Master Geoffrey had made.

"It's amazing, Ben. How on earth do you have the willpower to stick to your resolve of one page a day? I'm sure I couldn't."

"I made a promise to my beloved master. I will not go back on it."

"Aye. He loved you well it seems."

"And I loved him."

"How did you know that the book would get you out of trouble?"

"I don't think I did entirely. I simply trusted that my master would know what was going on and would write about it. That he wrote directly to the town reeve was..."

"Amazing," said Christa.

"Yes..." Bennet was almost in a dream.

"Do you mind if I lie down and sleep? I am so tired and pained."

Harry went down the stairs to let himself out. Once again Christa went to the front door to bolt it behind him.

"Best you take care, until the town reeve apprehends the villain."

"Yes. I will take good care of us both."

Harry nodded.

"And Harry?"

"Yes?"

"Not a word about me telling you that I love Bennet. I know that he is my master and cannot possibly return my love. So..."

"Ah...yes..."

"I don't want him to know how I feel..."

"You think he cannot possibly be in love with you?"

"No. He has said that he will be a celibate aesthete all his life. There's no place in his life for a woman, save as a servant."

"Ah...you're sure about that are you?"

She shrugged. He smiled and before he left said,

"You know, of course, that you have no document between you that says that you are simply his servant? That is something neither of you have yet accomplished."

When Christa returned to the upper room, Bennet was fast asleep.

*****

It was a fine late November day when the rime coated the roofs of the town houses and a light fog swirled around the marketplace.

Bennet had risen early to begin a chart for one of the great landowners of the county who wished to know if it was wise to add some rather geographically removed lands, to those he presently owned which were close by the town.

He took his astrolabe and plotted the position of the planets upon the day the lands would be transferred.

The moon gave the seeker the mind to make the right decision. Jupiter was the signifier of wealth and progress and Saturn was the planet responsible for destiny. Bennet puzzled over the alignments. They were all good.

Yes. January was perfect for this transaction. It would be successful if the lands were purchased and transferred upon the first to the fourth day of January. He wrote a missive to that effect and sealed it with his ring; his old master's ring which he'd discovered when Christa had been having one of her tidying up sessions, in the bottom of a chest. He looked at it carefully. Raised in the middle of the ring, was a piece of black onyx carved into the likeness of a star and a crescent moon. He thought it resembled the moon anyway.

He dribbled some wax onto the parchment and pressed the image carefully into it.

Then, taking his pen he dipped it into the ink and wrote the name of the addressee.

"Christa?"

She poked her head out of the stairwell.

"Might you find a lad to take this to the castle for me? It's to be dispatched to Salisbury."

"I'll see if I can find wee Johnnie. He'll do it for a bit of biscuit." She laughed, "he's always hungry."

She took the letter, threw on her cloak and stepped out of the house.

Once again it was market day and things were very busy.

Christa, threading her way across the road, eyed up the honey seller, and vowed to pass by there again on her way home. Honey was always a welcome ingredient in winter remedies and in cooking when warm, sweet comfort dishes were needed.

She raised her arm to Master Fletschier.

"Good day!"

She came alongside him. "Master Fletschier. Is your little lad here? I have a commission for him from Master Celest."

"Ah yes. He's in the alleyway. Go round."

Christa found the young lad and asked him to run to the castle to take the missive to the office of the messengers and that if he would return by the astrologer's house there would be a reward for him. The lad grinned a happy, seven year old toothless grin and ran off.

Christa turned back to the honey seller.

"Mistress Christa. How wonderful to see you again."

It was Master Milling, looking thinner than he had previously been; his face was sunken and he had a pallor like the flour with which he worked.

Christa was surprised.

"Master Milling. I heard you'd been ill. Are you not yet recovered?"

"It's a slow process but yes. I feel much better thank you."

"I heard that you lost your mother to this awful contagion."

"Aye...aye I did. She was never well, you understand and it was no surprise that she was taken with it."

"Please accept my sincere..."

"In a way it was a mercy for she had been failing for a while. She was suffering terribly."

"Aw... how awful." Christa crossed herself. "God take her to His Bosom."

"How are you? You look very well and if I may say it, very lovely today."

"That is kind of you to say so."

"Not at all, it's the truth."

Christa purchased some honey from the apiarist and turned to walk home.

"Mistress, might I call upon you later? I wondered if you might like to walk out with me by the river?"

"I have no washing to do, Master Milling," giggled Christa.

Benedict Milling smiled. "Ah yes...it was where we first met wasn't it? It seems an age ago."

Christa looked earnestly at this young man. How old was he? Twenty four, five? Out of his apprenticeship as a miller and into the journeyman stage. Christa knew that he worked at the town mill. There would be no place for him there as a master, for she knew that Master Grist was the main miller besides Master Barbflet, the owner. One day, Benedict would move on and find a mill of his own. Then he would be a good catch for a girl.

'If he could put some flesh on him - he would be handsome,' she said to herself. Indeed she remembered him on the day she'd met him. Strong, broad shouldered, and fatter in the face with a cheeky grin and forward nature. Now he seemed, cowed and subdued, quieter.

Would she like to go out to walk with him? Why not?

It was certain that her love for her master was not to be returned. It was obvious Master Milling was fond of her. Could she not get fond of him in time?

'I will not know it, until I give it a chance,' she said to herself.

"I would like that very much. I will be finished with my chores at around midday."

"Then I will call for you." He took her elbow.

"You aren't walking out with anyone else...are you...I'd hate to..."

"No."

He accompanied her back to the house and as they approached the door, it was opened by an unseen hand.

"Do come in," said a voice. Christa said thank you to Master Milling and stepped over the threshold.

She closed the door and turned.

Amazingly, Bennet was standing stiffly side by side with Mistress Alleyn in the consulting room. The door to the work room was open.

"Oh," said Christa, putting down her honey, "I'm sorry I had no idea you had a visitor." She swung off her cloak. "It's nice to see you mistress."

Christa had thought she'd never see this woman set foot in the house again, after what had happened but here she was looking at Master Celest with a studied air.

No...there was something wrong. It wasn't a natural stare.

"Agh..." said the woman in a strangled tone. Her eyes swivelling to the open door of the workroom behind her.

"Are you alright?" asked Christa.

She stepped forward to offer assistance.

It was then she noticed the noose around the woman's neck and the ropes around her wrists.

Through the doorway of the work room came a figure dressed in dark blue.

"Christa! Nice to see you again. I've been looking for you."

CHAPTER FOURTEEN ~ CAPTURE

"**B**asketwright!"

The man yanked on the rope which was tight around Mistress Alleyn's neck. The poor woman moaned in fear.

"Let her go. What is she to you?"

"I am afraid I came in here looking for your master and of course for you. Your master, I found."

He pulled on a second rope and Bennet stepped backwards with a gurgle. He too was trussed up.

"Sadly this other woman came into the shop as I was just about to string up your master from his own house beam. Oh how sad. Taken his own life. Couldn't live with what he'd done. So here she is."

"Still murdering? Just add another to your tally eh?" said Christa.

"Well. You'll do just as well."

Basketwright took the rope from Bennet's neck and pushed him to the other side of the room.

"In fact. It's you I really want. He would always have been second best."

Christa noticed he had a long knife in his right hand and the two ends of the rope in his left.

He motioned that Christa come closer.

She stepped up.

"No!" cried Bennet, "No Christa."

Christa saw there were tears in Bennet's eyes.

"It's always been about me, Master Bennet," she said. "You will have no peace until he has me."

"No!"

Mistress Alleyn whimpered, totally confused by all this.

"Let her go," said Bennet. "She has nothing to do with this."

"I will do as you wish," said Christa, "if you let her go."

Basketwright laughed as he put the noose around Christa's neck. A forced sound which went on a little too long for sincerity.

"I tell you what...make a choice Master Astrologer. It seems I cannot do what I wished today. I am going to walk out of here and away safely and wait for another opportunity to silence you. You know too much. You both know too much. But I can wait. I don't want any other witnesses. You two are enough. And I have no wish to hurt the lady."

"You chose the wrong time. Market day...it's far too busy," said Bennet, "people will see you."

"Ah no. Everyone will be busy and about their own tasks. I will simply exit your property and for my own security I am going to take a hostage with me. You will not follow or I swear I will kill."

Bennet licked his lips.

"Leave them...please...take me."

The man shook his head.

"And deprive myself of the pleasure of making you squirm?" he grinned.

"Choose, Master Apothecary... choose. Which is it to be? Whom shall I free? Mistress Alleyn, or Christa?

Bennet remained silent.

"Aw come on, we can't wait all day. Shall I prod you a little." The man stuck the knife into Christa's back and she squealed.

"I'll count to three. Christa or Mistress Alleyn. What *is* your name madam?"

His prisoner turned to look at him for the first time, terror written all over her face, "Agnes," she whispered tremulously.

"So, Agnes...or Christa?"

"I'll count to three... one...two...thre..."

"Agnes!" blurted Bennet.

Basketwright grinned. "Oh dear, Christa. Your master doesn't love you as much as he loves this other woman."

Christa's heart fell to her feet.

Basketwright secured the noose around Christa's neck even tighter, and eventually pulled the rope from Mistress Alleyn's neck. He pushed her towards Bennet.

"Now unlock the door."

"It is unlocked."

"Give me the key..." It would not occur to the basket maker that Christa might also have a key. She was a servant. Servants were not trusted with keys.

Bennet removed his key from his purse and held it out. He did not mention the other key.

Dragging Christa with him, the felon shut the shutters, bolted them and with the hilt end of his knife he struck the bolt from the metal fastener. One sheared, the other bent.

Then he dragged Christa backwards to the door and opened it.

"Say goodbye. You probably won't see her alive again." He tightened his grip and brought Christa closely to his side, like a lover giving an embrace.

They stepped together out into the market crowds.

*****

Master Milling was watching the door of the astrologer's house, as he had done countless times over the past few months, waiting for a glimpse of Christa.

There was no point in him going from here, for midday was but a short time away and he had promised Christa he would see her then.

He was surprised, therefore, to see her come out so quickly after he'd spoken to her, without the warmth of her cloak and in company with a man. Close company.

'Oh… was this someone for whom she had an affection?' They were certainly familiar and close. The man had his hand upon the small of her back and also around her neck, as if he would caress her.

Benedict looked away. No, surely she would not lie to him. And where were they going?

Midday was a short time away. Would she be back to meet him?

He decided to follow.

As he followed and reached the outskirts of town, he realised with a shock, that the man held a knife to Christa's back and guided her in her walking with a rope around her neck, like a performing animal.

"Odd," he said aloud. "Not the action of a lover."

He followed further out of town.

*****

Bennet sprang into action as soon as the man had closed and locked the door. The door was not going to be able to be opened, for Master Lockyer had made that impossible, from the outside or inside, without a key.

It wasn't going to be possible to shatter the planks either for it was sturdy and fixed with metal.

He used his teeth to slacken the knots in his bindings and threw them away. Then he untied poor Mistress Alleyn.

Bennet tried the shutters. He prised them apart but, again they held. All he did was graze his finger ends and break his nails.

"Mistress Alleyn, you must stay here and rest yourself until I return….or maybe you can call from the upstairs window for someone to aid you."

"Where will you be?" said the little woman rubbing her throat.

"I am going to try to exit through the larger upstairs window." The small window in the work room was no size and Bennet would never be able to squeeze through it.

"What?"

"I shall break it apart until I am able to get through."

He bounded upstairs in three leaps and made the first floor window of the parlour room. This was unshuttered at this time of day. Bennet looked round for something to use. A three legged stool was the first item he laid eyes upon.

With great vigour and a certain amount of anger, he threw himself at the window bars, hitting them with all his might.

One shattered. He took hold of the edge and pulled mightily. He noticed that Agnes Alleyn had accompanied him upstairs and was watching from the second step, like a timid mouse peeping from a hole.

The bar came away bringing with it a deal of the wattle and daub of which the wall was made.

Another attempt at the bars with the stool failed to produce anything. Bennet gritted his teeth and swung with all his might. A piece of the central bar went flying into the room.

One more swing and he'd made a gap in the window big enough to crawl through. Three out of the five bars were gone.

He threw down the now ruined stool.

"Mistress, call from the window, tell people what has happened, get the town reeve to send after me... And hand me my quarterstaff ...it's there by the window."

He pulled off his supertunic and bundled it on the table and threw the staff from the window. Going out backwards, holding onto the remaining frame, he eased his legs over the cill and dropped.

Mistress Alleyn called after him,

"Where are you going?"

"I don't know," was the reply."

*****

Christa made life difficult for the basket maker. She pulled back, she bit, she kicked. This resistance just earned her a tighter noose so that she could barely breathe and a pricked back full of injuries.

They walked at first as tightly jammed together as they could possibly be. After they'd left the marketplace, he allowed her a little leeway and that's when she tried to fight.

"Where are we going?"

"To where I was living after the wife...died..."

"You killed her you mean."

"Aye...after I killed her. I have a little place, just a hut you understand, where I have bits of food and a few weapons. I can hole up there for ages. No one knows about it."

"Not even Mistress Ferrers."

"Not even that bitch."

"They'll be looking for you..."

"Well I'll just disappear, like I've done before. Now move on."

They were running up the Granham Hill, the road which led eventually to Pewsey. This road was an often used highway for both people on foot and in carts.

They met one or two people, latecomers to the market but no one exchanged the time of day with them.

Staring straight ahead, Basketwright managed to pass them without any interaction.

Christa was breathless with running and it was even harder to breathe with the tightness of the noose around her neck.

"Please...can we stop...? I can't breathe."

But he allowed her no respite.

"For someone who is going to die anyway when I am safe, you worry about how you'll breathe now... PAH!"

All at once they veered off the main road and onto a mere grassy track which led into trees; outliers of Savernake Forest.

"Not long now..." the man laughed. "Say your prayers."

*****

Master Milling kept the pair in sight. Luckily, the felon did not look back. Benedict tried to remain hidden as much as possible but it wasn't easy, especially upon the Granham Hill for there were fewer large trees here.

He saw the pair veer off into the greenery of Savernake and knew that he must not let them out of sight or he would be lost. Christa would be lost, for it was obvious the man meant her harm.

'What on earth is going on,' he said to himself, 'and who *is* this man?'

He felt for the knife at his hip. If he had to defend Christa, he would. He loved her. He would do anything for her, even lay down his life.

He followed into the trees and tried to watch how he trod so that noise of pursuit would not alert the man.

Christa and her captor travelled further into the wood and at last they reached a small glade. Master Milling peering around, could see no one. They had suddenly and completely disappeared.

*****

Bennet gathered his wits as soon as he hit the ground. Which way had they gone? He had not seen.

Surely they would not go further into town, he reckoned. Where would the man take her...back to the cottage? No, that was too obvious. But he would go out of town, that much he knew. He turned down the High Street and ran past St. Peter's, breathing a prayer as he jogged.

There were few people on that road but one man with a long staff and a pack on his back was coming along the Pewsey Road.

"A man and a girl... travelling together... closely together. Have you seen them?"

The man looked him up and down.

"Run away with a lover has she?"

"She's been abducted…"

"Up the Granham Hill. I saw them a while back. Thought something was odd."

"Thank you" yelled Bennet as he ran on.

Up the hill, which was quite steep he ploughed on, his lungs bursting. In his head the words, 'I will never forgive myself,' kept repeating and repeating in time with his running steps.

"Oh Christa my love. My little wren. Where are you?"

He had to stop for a few heartbeats to catch his breath. He was not used to such exertion. Ahead of him, he saw a figure. A lone figure in a yellow, green cotte travelling fast westward.

Had not Master Milling dressed in yellow green the other day, when Bennet had spied him watching Christa from across the road. He thought back to the feeling which ran through him when he'd seen the man.

It was not pleasant. Jealousy. He told himself that he had no right to be jealous. If Master Milling was wanting to court Christa then it was up to him. And her.

Nevertheless the sight of him now, made his blood heat and he ran on faster.

Should he call out? *Was* the man following? It was likely, for Bennet knew that Master Milling was often to be found watching for Christa in the hope she'd come out of the house. Sometimes he was lucky and she'd walk about the marketplace with him. Bennet realised that he too had been spying on Christa and felt terrible about it.

"Master Milling!"

The man did not hear him.

"Benedict!" yelled Bennet, cupping his mouth.

The man turned.

*****

Christa stumbled into a pit dug in the forest floor. Basketwright had made himself a shelter of twigs and branches covered over with leaves and fronds of the bracken. He was after all a basket weaver and was good at plaiting together natural materials. At this time of year, it was indistinguishable from the colours and textures of the forest and blended in wonderfully.

She fell to her knees and the rope around her neck tightened again. She pulled on it to loosen it.

"Ah no you don't."

Basketwright hauled her up, took off the noose and, bringing her hands around to her waist, he bound her tightly with rope.

"And just so you can't call out." He wrapped a filthy rag around her mouth and tied it tight.

"No one ever comes here. It's a forgotten part of the forest. So no one will rescue you."

A beefy branch was threaded from one side of the little shelter to the other and Basketwright threw the rope over it hauling Christa from the ground so that her toe tips just touched the earth. A searing pain went through her shoulder as her arms were pulled above her head. He fixed the end of the rope to a spike in the ground and began to empty the place of food and weapons which he had previously stashed there. Stuffing them into a pannier, the man muttered to himself.

"I had thought to kill you; cut yer throat maybe, a wound to the heart perhaps, hang you even...but now I think I'll just leave you here to rot. That's better than you deserve. If you die of hunger and thirst, then I can't be accused of your murder now can I?"

Christa wriggled but it just served to tighten the rope. Her wrists were burning.

"Yeah! Food for the forest animals...eventually...that's fitting."

He ducked out of the structure calling, "Goodbye Christa, you'll need those prayers now."

Christa screamed with all her might. But hardly any sound came out of her dry mouth.

*****

Benedict and Bennet met in the middle of the green track to the forest just inside the mass of trees. Bennet puffed out a huge sigh and gradually got his breath back.

"Master Milling…"

"Ben please…"

"Ben… I hope you are following Christa and her captor?"

"Aye…who is the man? Why has he taken her?"

"No time to explain now… Where are they?" whispered Bennet.

Benedict pointed, "in that glade there. You can just see it. I stepped back to see if I had missed something. I lost them, about there."

The two men crept forward.

If Basketwright had not exited his shelter of twigs just at that moment, his pannier slung over his back, they might never have found the cleverly hidden den.

Benedict started forward but Bennet held him back.

"Surely he will fight…? Best we make sure Christa is alright first… yes?" he whispered.

Bennet's anger with Basketwright made him want to pursue and kill the man with his bare hands, but he knew that, even with his trusty staff, he was unlikely to come off best.

"But he'll get away!"

"If he has harmed her, then the two of us follow him and exact our revenge. He won't get too far too fast in territory like this," said Bennet.

The miller realised that Bennet was much clearer headed than he was, much cooler.

"Quickly!"

Once the man had disappeared amongst the nearer trees, they

crept towards the hut. Bennet's heart was pounding. 'Oh please...let her live...if wounded...let her be alive. Please.' He didn't hold out much hope.

What a surprise for both Christa and the men when they entered the hut.

Christa had been trying to break the hold which the large branch had on the side wall of the structure. She realised that if she bounced up and down hard enough, the outer casing would buckle and disintegrate. It had been hard work upon her wrists which were bloodied and scraped by the harshness of the rope, but she was achieving a degree of success.

"Christa!"

Master Celest entered first and pushing past, Milling gave a joyous cry, "Oh you are alright. Thanks be to God!"

At that moment the branch broke and Christa tumbled with it to the floor of the hut. Her arms ached enormously and her wrists were bleeding.

Master Milling scooped her up and held her to his breast.

"Oh Christa I was so afraid."

"Mmot arf mush as I wo," said Christa against her gag. This was supposed to mean 'not half as much as I was.'

"Take off the gag, Ben," said Bennet, a surge of relief passing through him.

He bent down and began to chafe her numbed hands.

"Oh Christa...I am so sorry this has happened to you."

Christa was cool to him. "I am alive at least."

Bennet noticed that Christa did not pull away from Master Milling but allowed him to stroke her hair and whisper endearments.

'So it has gone thus far?' he said to himself and straightened up.

All thoughts of pursuing Basketwright gone, they gathered Christa up from the floor and together half carried her outside into the glade.

"Our first priority must be to get Mistress Wren to the doctor," said Bennet, "And then to report this crime to your master."

On the way home, stumbling and struggling, for all of them were tired by the escapade, Bennet and Christa told Milling the story of the murder of Mistress Margaret, the actions of the two hoaxing criminals and the vindictiveness of Mistress Ferrers. Then they came to the death of Ferrers at the hands of Basketwright.

"Ah... I have a friend who has fallen foul of them."

"You have...? Would they be willing to testify in front of the sheriff's officer?"

"I don't know. He did pay the pair money to keep quiet. They were going to tell his wife."

"And he told no one...but you?"

"I advised him to go to the authorities but he said that Lecia, his wife would be horrified and he just couldn't risk it."

"It's not just the lechery of the men," said Christa, "It's the reputation of their wives

in the town which keep folk silent."

"What do you mean?"

"Who wants anyone to know that their husband has been taken in and led by the front of his braies?"

Bennet felt quite uncomfortable.

*****

Christa's wounds salved and her torn and muddied clothes changed, she brushed her hair and noted how much it had grown in the intervening months.

Bennet and Ben had gone to the town reeve to explain what had happened.

And Christa was alone with the door firmly locked with her key.

Of course the main problem now, was the ruined window. That had to be boarded up for the time being and made safe.

There was a call at the outer door.

"Mistress! William Cartwright. Come to mend your window."

"Ah yes. This was a friend of Bennet's. Although the man actually worked in the wagon yard, he was perfectly able to do the woodwork required to mend the window.

Christa called down from the intact window.

"Please, come in and do what you need to do."

She peered down at the man, who waved to her. 'Oh...would she now have to spend the rest of her days worrying about who was at the door of the house?' She let him in.

With Master Cartwright in the house, Christa felt a little safer and she retreated to her curtained cubbyhole and looked at her ruined brown cotte. She would have to patch and sew it, in order to wear it again; she'd look like a beggar. It was ruined.

What was wrong with her? She could settle to nothing. She tried some finger braiding but the colours would not obey her. She took up her needle to sew but realised that her hands were still too damaged. She took up a parchment which Bennet had left in the main room and read aloud,

'But Iseult answered, "No, you know that you are my lord and my master, and I your slave. Ah, why did I not salve those wounds of the wounded singer, or let die that dragon-killer in the grasses of the marsh? But then I did not know what I know now!"

"And what is it that you know, Iseult?"

She laid her arm upon Tristan's shoulder, the light of her eyes was drowned and her lips trembled.

"The love of you," she said. Whereupon he put his lips to hers.'

'What was this? Had Bennet written it?' She read on...

'The lovers held each other tight; life and desire trembled through their youthful bodies, and Tristan said, "Well then, come to me, Death."

And as evening fell, upon the boat that heeled and ran to King Mark's land, they gave themselves up wholly to love.'

Christa gulped. Some kind of story about lovers. She went back to the beginning to read more. These lovers were illicit it seemed.

Unlikely to survive the wrath of King Mark, whoever he was.

She sat down to read the whole poem.

She finished the last line;

'And when she had turned to the east and prayed to God, she moved the body of her beloved Tristan and lay down by the dead man. She kissed his mouth and his face, and clasped him closely; and so gave up her soul, and died beside him of grief for love.'

Her eyes streamed with tears and her heart was aching.

'Oh that was so beautiful.'

Barely had she had time to put the parchment down and dry her eyes than the master astrologer and Benedict Milling hollered to be let in.

"The sheriff will send out a party to the constable and warden of the forest. They'll be on the lookout for the beast," said Bennet.

"And the warden will comb the forest," added Master Milling. "If he's there, they'll find him."

"He has managed to evade them before," said Christa sniffing. "He's a wily fox."

"He thinks you are dead. His problems are over…"

"Ah no, Bennet. You remember he said he would bide his time and come after *you*."

The men looked at each other.

"I think that he will have the sense to stay away," said Benedict. "He's a wanted man."

"And has been for some time," said Christa. "But he's been under the noses of us all for months. Forgive me; you don't know him like I do. He likes to make people suffer."

She came forward to pour them ale. "Do we know how poor mistress Alleyn is?"

"None the worse for her ordeal. She has told the town reeve what happened. It was unfortunate that she happened to come in just as Basketwright was about to perform his evil deed. Lucky for me though, that she followed me through the door when she did."

"He would not kill her. Did you notice?" said Ben. "Why was that do you think?

Christa turned her back on Bennet and did not answer Ben.

"Maybe he has some conscience after all," said Bennet.

"Asked to choose, you chose her?"

Christa turned and gave the astrologer a cup. "Why?"

"Why did I choose to free her and not you?" said Bennet with a gulp.

"Yes...what is she to you?"

Bennet put the cup down. "Christa..."

"I think I shall be going, said Master Milling with an embarrassed grin. "I have things to do," and without further word, he drained his cup and clomped down the stairs. They heard the door close.

"Why did you choose her above me? You know me better. We have lived together in this house..."

"Christa... please."

"She means more to you than I do."

"That's not true."

"You exchanged her for me."

"She doesn't mean more to me than you. It was just that... she has children...you do not. In that tense breath of a moment, I thought of her boys being motherless, that's all."

Christa squirmed and her facial expression moved from resentment to mortification as she thought about the repercussions of Mistress Alleyn's death.

"Ah well..." she turned away so that he might not see her discomfort.

"And she has already lost her mother and a child..."

"Well then, if I am to survive in the world...I need to have children. I will remember that next time my life is in danger."

"Well it can be organised."

Christa tried to ignore him but her heart started to beat just a little faster.

"You might marry Master Milling. There is no doubt that he loves you."

Christa swallowed hard.

"What if I do not love him."

"Do you?"

Christa slumped on a chair. "I don't know... No I don't. I don't think I do."

"Well then you must not marry him for you once said to me that you'd only marry for love."

Christa looked deeply into his eyes. "A love as profound as that of Tristan and Iseult?"

He chuckled. "Ah, I see you have been reading."

"Did you write that story?"

Bennet threw back his head and laughed in true mirth. "Goodness me, no. I have not that much...romance in me. Or imagination."

"Then who?"

"A poet long ago, so long ago we do not know how old the story is."

"It's very sad."

"It is...but I suppose that is what comes of using magic to achieve one's ambition. There is always something to repay. A love philtre which makes the two fall for each other? Never a good idea."

Christa blushed to her hairline. "Oh, please, by all the saints, please tell me that he does not know....what I did."

"You would rather go by your charts and comparisons to see if folk are compatible and if they can fall in love?"

"Well...I *can* say that it works. And that it is against no one's will."

"No."

There was an uncomfortable silence.

"I have done no work today. I suppose I must, if I can concentrate. Are you sure you're alright?"

"I bought some honey earlier today, I shall retrieve it and do some cooking for the festivities."

He smiled sweetly at her. As sweet as the honey she'd bought.

"Do not do anything you do not need to do. You have had a terrible day."

Again, here he was being so kind and thoughtful. Christa's heart constricted.

"I think it will do me good to be busy."

*****

Bennet went back over the pages of his book that evening. The day of his arrest by the town reeve and the death of the woman Ferrers, whom he now knew was called Jehanne.

'You will be reading this aloud, Master Barbflet and Bennet will have no knowledge of what I write, for he will not yet have been able to read this. He has been in some danger, which is not yet past. The young wren too, is in danger. He is guiltless of any error, save that of being over fond of his fellow man and poking his nose in where he feels he can be of help.'

He turned the page.

'Basketwright is a violent man. However, the killing of his wife was an unfortunate accident, as was the death of the woman who was found yesterday. No doubt the basket maker is guilty of both deaths but it was not out and out murder.'

This was the page which the town reeve had read to himself. Bennet read the next page. The following day's prognostication.

'However it will be murder if the basket maker manages to silence the wren as he wishes. Great care must be taken. Once again, grasp the nettle Bennet. Do not procrastinate. Take what you want before another steals it from you.'

Why had he not the courage to declare his feelings. Was he afraid of being laughed at...ridiculed?

He lay awake that night thinking about Christa and how he would, at the first opportunity, ask her to marry him.

Christa, alone in her cubbyhole was awake too. Oh how she wished she could just tell him how she felt. She had been so close to it...but it didn't seem right when they had been talking about Mistress Alleyn and the miller.

Yes, tomorrow she would say something and, before she fell asleep, she rehearsed the very words she would say to Bennet, the master astrologer.

CHAPTER FIFTEEN
THE WREN HUNT

A flurry of work came in just before Christmas and Bennet was very busy with charts for legal cases, monies and properties transferred to new owners and with natal charts for several people who wished to marry in January, a popular time for weddings.

He thought about his own declaration of love and *his* wedding and put it to the back of his mind. Plenty of time over the days of Christmas when he would have a whole twelve days off, to ask Christa to marry him.

Christa too put off her declaration. He was still showing no real sign of being interested in her and so she changed her mind again and walked out with Master Milling.

"Shall we go to the wren hunt on St. Stephen's Day?" said Ben on the Sunday before Christmas.

"The beating of the bounds?" said Christa, idling along the riverside at the water meadow to the south of the town mill.

"Well that too. It's both. The boundary of the town is beaten with sticks and at the same time, the wrens are chased from their hiding places."

"I always thought it sad that such a tiny bird had to be so hunted," said Christa.

"It's traditional," said Milling. "One dead wren will be fixed to a

219

pole and decorated with straw and greenery."

"I have never seen it."

"Oh it's a good day, believe me," said Ben. "Dancing and singing and drinking. The whole town joins in."

"So where do they begin?"

"In the marketplace. And then they walk up the road to St. Mary's…"

"Singing and drinking…?"

"More or less. And then they go down the hill to the bridge all the time beating the bushes and trees and other markers." Master Milling began to sing.

"The wren, the wren is king of the birds,

St. Stephen's Day was caught in the furze,

Although he is little his family is great,

We pray you, good people to give us a treat.

Come out with the money…"

"Oh there's money involved is there?" said Christa jokingly.

"It's collected from householders and well-wishers as they go along and it all goes to the church," said Milling, picking up a branch and swishing the dying plants growing by the river.

"So the crowd goes round the whole town?"

"Yes, from the marketplace to the church, down to the bridge and along the Newbury road. Then they turn up by the castle bridge, beat their way up the hill to the common, along Back Lane and eventually to Herd Street and back to the marketplace again.

"I suspect quite a lot of alcohol can be consumed on such a perambulation?" said Christa playfully.

"Gets a bit unruly some years…yes." said Ben with a laugh. "But there are always those who keep order; the priest and town reeve and some men from the castle, to make sure it all goes smoothly."

"And this is all so we know where the town boundaries are…lest we forget?"

"It's been happening for so many years. No one can recall a year when it didn't happen."

"So why a wren?"

Benedict chuckled. "I don't know, save the feathers of a wren protect you from drowning."

"Do they indeed? And do you know of anyone who has been protected in this way?"

Ben pursed his lips and fingered his chin.

"Do you know…? I don't."

"But if you worked on the water, fishermen and the like, you'd be a fool not to have the odd feather on you all the time?"

"Just in case. And new ones every year are needed."

"It's a very good job that there are a lot of wrens."

Ben, swishing his branch, started to chase Christa. "I have heard they're quite easy to catch."

She giggled and ran off in the direction of the town bridge.

He caught her just as she scrambled up the bank. He'd let go of his encumbering branch and caught her around the waist. She giggled and laughed.

He folded her into his arms and pressed his cold lips to hers. She closed her eyes, not knowing what to expect, for this was the first time ever a man had kissed her properly.

The girls she knew all told her that the first kiss was amazing. She would feel hot and bothered, but nicely so. Her heart would pound and shivers would go up and down her spine. They told her that she would not be able to let go, that she would want the moment to last forever; that if the kiss persisted it would send a fire through her veins and a strange feeling in her chest and then her loins.

That was when you were supposed to stop and let go.

Christa felt…nothing. Just the cold wet pressure of Master Benedict's soft lips on hers.

She pulled away. He turned and leaned on the rail of the bridge.

"I'm sorry. I should not have done that. It was unforgivable. I should have asked you first."

"No... no... it was...a spur of the moment thing," said Christa, trying to make light of the instant.

She looked up at the sky. "I think it will be a fine Christmas Day, do you?"

"Let's hope it's a fine St. Stephen's day."

"What are you doing on Christmas Day? Where will you be?"

"At my sister's and her husband's house on St. Martin's. She and my mother didn't get on. That was why I stayed at home, to look after my mother. But when she was gone, I managed to convince my sister that my mother had been the problem and not me. My mother never accepted my sister's marriage, you see."

"You were estranged but now you are reconciled?"

"That's right. She will be at the hunting, with her two young boys. Shall I introduce you?"

Christa held her breath. For a young man to introduce a young lady to his family...well, that might mean serious business.

"As long as you tell them we are simply friends."

He reached for her hand. "Of course."

*****

Christa and Bennet went to mass on Christmas Eve. She always loved the feel of the Christ's mass - that one service specially sung for the birth of Christ at midnight.

The church was decked out with greenery and all the finest candlesticks, silver, robes and altar cloths were pressed into service. Her eyes feasted on the finery as she listened to the words the priest chanted in the chancel, solely reserved for him and his helpers. The church was packed, even into the darkest corners which folk usually avoided. It was quite a mild night and they dawdled along the High afterwards, speaking to folk they knew, wishing them a Merry Christmas, knowing that they would be seeing them again in the morning for the Christmas Day service and doing it all over again.

Christa looked up at Bennet, wearing his master's green hood. He looked very magisterial in it and Christa's heart gave a little leap. Why did the face of this rather ordinary man send her heart into such rhythms? Why did she have a desperate need to touch him, to be near to him? To smile at him and laugh with him. Be happy.

And yet, the handsome face of Master Milling did absolutely nothing to her. She'd tried. Oh how hard she had tried, but no matter how often she had examined the bones and contours of the miller's face, his good, clear skin, his deep brown eyes, the broad shoulders and muscles of his arms, his narrow hips and shapely legs, her heart had never fluttered, as it did when her master came into the room.

She put it to the back of her mind and gave herself over to Christmas.

A day later the town was buzzing with activity. The marketplace became like a town fair. People were milling about, greeting friends and neighbours. Drinking began early, folk carrying their ale and cider in leather flasks and bottles. There was an air of an outdoor party with people sharing food and special Christmas treats. Christa stepped out of the house warmly wrapped in her cloak, for the weather had turned chilly overnight.

Master Milling met her at the door.

"They will wait a little longer. No one has yet caught the wren which will be fixed to the pole. The young lads are out now beating the bushes on the Pewsey Road. It won't be long."

"Poor little thing," said Christa with a heartfelt sigh.

Bennet Celest came out of his door and locked it.

"Good day Master Milling. May the blessing of St. Stephen be with you this day."

"And may God pour down his blessings upon you Master Astrologer, in this joyous season. You are joining us then, for the hunt?"

"When I was younger, I was part of the hunt. Apprentices, I think, make up the greater number of the hunters. You have never joined in the hunt, Benedict?"

"No. I have always been in the crowd which follows."

"Well now, I too will be part of the appreciative crowd."

They hung around for a further hour until a great shout went up from the greenery around the churchyard of St. Peter's.

They had captured a wren.

The boys and young men paraded a pole which was garnished with shiny green holly, ivy leaves and the flowers of the ivy. A few berries clung to the holly twigs and shone like little drops of blood.

Straw had been fixed to the underside of the greenery atop the pole and over it all dangled the tiny corpse of a spread winged wren.

Christa watched as they walked past her, the pole held aloft by one of the roper's young fourteen year old apprentices, grinning like a dog with two tails.

"Did you ever hold the pole?" asked Christa of Bennet as the apprentice passed them.

"Aye one year. I was fifteen, I think. It's a great honour. But by the end of it, you have a sore head"

Now the pole was paraded around the marketplace and everyone cheered and whistled. Some folk started to sing,

"Where are you going? said Richard to Robin,

Where are you going? said Dibyn to Dobyn,

Where are you going? said John,

Where are you going? said the Never Beyond."

Christa chuckled. "What does it all mean?"

"I think the words have been lost over the centuries and all we have now is some sort of doggerel made up of what was once probably a spell or magical incantation," said Bennet.

"Oh?" This was Master Milling. "I heard that the thing probably originated with the druids of old, in their arcane magic. Who knows what it really meant?"

"Oh. They're off..."said Christa, putting forward her best foot. "Up to the church I think."

Christa, with Milling's arm through her left and Bennet's through her right, marched up the marketplace in the middle of the crowd.

"Why does it have to be a wren?" asked Christa.

"Well, many, many years ago," began Master Milling, "the story goes that all the birds gathered together and wanted to have a king. The birds were satisfied that the bird that would fly the highest was to *be* their king."

"So all the birds flew up into the air and the eagle far above them looked down and shouted, "I am the king of all birds." But the wren hopping out from beneath the eagle's wing shouted "You are not the king yet," and he flew still higher," added Bennet.

"The eagle was too tired to follow him and the wily wren was declared the king," said Master Milling.

"But when the wren came down out of the air the birds said he was too small and they proposed to drown him. But no water was to be found so all the birds began to cry into a bowl. When the bowl was filled with tears, the clumsy owl tripped over the bowl and spilled it. They had all their tears shed and had nothing to drown him and so he's still the king of all birds."

"Oh that's a lovely story," said Christa. "To think I am named after such a clever bird!"

Then all three ran up the alleyway to the church jostled by the crowd at knee and elbow.

The crowd stopped in the churchyard and the young lad who held the pole was relieved of it.

"Here now young Philip!" shouted one of the town elders, grabbing hold of the lad's head.

"Into your head goes the first marker," and he banged the lad's head against a fence post which was situated at the side of the yard.

A stick was procured and off they went, beating the hedges and smaller trees, whooping and yelling and singing the 'wren song' at the top of their voices.

The second stop was on Barn Street, by the town green. The poor lad with the pole was seized again and this time his head was banged against an old yew tree which had stood in this place from time immemorial.

"The second marker goes in your head," shouted the old man and the lad shook his locks and took up his pole again.

"He'll have a sore head come the end of the day," said Christa.

"Aye I know it," laughed Bennet, "I too had a bruised head."

"This is all so that the markers may be driven into the memory is it?"

"One way to do it." said Master Milling, chuckling.

The crowd surged forward down the road and onto the town bridge over the river Kennet where the young lad was once more set to knock the information into his memory.

One of their neighbours offered Bennet and Christa a drink from a leather flask but they declined. Some people were becoming quite tipsy now.

"The wren, the wren is the king of the birds..."

By now Christa had got the gist of the song and was singing happily along with the rest. She still had her arm through Master Celest's but had somehow relinquished Ben's hold. He did not seem to mind, being involved with a group of young men at a singing match, it seemed.

Christa looked up at Bennet. He was happily watching everything. People passing, the dancing couples, the snaking groups of dancers flowing back and forth along the road. He laughed at a couple of lads taken short with their drink, as they hid in the bushes to relieve their bladders.

Down the Newbury Road the revellers went. Here a boulder was pressed into service as a marker.

They came to the edge of the castle bridge where the Newbury road met the Pewsey road. Here there were many bushes by the river and several venerable old Willows like magicians with long beards, leaned out over the water, many of the leaves still being present on the trees. Here it was the stones of the bridge itself which became the boundary marker and Philip was once more relieved of his pole and forced to his knees whilst his head was touched, (they were a little more careful now), to the stone. The rhyme was chanted again.

Bennet and Christa were loitering at the back of the crowd, watching a dog that had appeared from nowhere, trying to worry the pole which the substitute wren boy was holding.

He held it as high as he could but the dog was a good jumper and the lad only about eight years of age.

"Get down Brun! You shan't have it," yelled the lad, half laughing, half crying.

Bennet leapt forward, "Here lad, give it to me, I'm taller than you."

The young boy relinquished the pole with a pout, realising that he alone was not going to be able to deter the dog.

Bennet held it high, laughing and joking with the animal.

Suddenly an arrow came whizzing out of nowhere and struck the wren pole above Bennet's head, sticking in the straw.

The astrologer had not noticed that the pole had been hit and was still leaping about with the dog.

Christa, however, being a little further away, saw exactly what had happened.

She yelled above the noise, "Bennet take care!"

She ran towards him, just as another arrow sped out of the bushes by the bridge. This one missed its target and went skittering out over the gravelly road.

Now others had realised that there were arrows being released haphazardly into the crowd. Screaming, family groups drew closer to each other, friends clutched arms and looked round.

Christa put herself in front of Bennet and scoured the bushes to see if she could see the bowman.

No one was visible.

Some folk ran away across the bridge, others milled about not quite understanding what to do or what was happening.

One of the older gentlemen of the town, Christa thought the man was a roper, walked forward bravely to see if he could see anyone.

"Come out you idiot! This is no joke! Someone could be hurt."

There was no answer and Master Roper looked back to the throng as if for help.

Christa turned and seizing Bennet by the front of his supertunic cried, "Is it Basketwright, do you think?"

Bennet shook his head. "Some drunken idiot, I suppose, making a fool of himself."

With the furore dying down, and no one hurt, many revellers began to move off the bridge and onto the road which ran between the castle, and the King's garden.

A few people were left puzzling over the odd incident and Bennet handed his pole back to the wren boy, who pulled out the arrow.

"Daft...daft thing to do," he said. "It's already dead. Can't kill it twice."

They were all of them almost across the bridge when a stentorian voice called out.

"Basketwright! Come out you coward!"

Bennet and Christa, closely followed by Master Milling, the roper and few others, turned back.

Their eyes searched the area but could not see anyone.

"Basketwright, you bastard! Come out and face me!"

"That's Pike, Jonas Pike," said one of the town blacksmiths. "I'd know his tones anywhere."

Another man looked puzzled. "Where the Hell has he been this past few weeks?"

The other man shrugged. "I thought he'd left town."

"We too wondered where he'd gone," said Bennet.

Now several men were combing the riverside bushes for the culprit.

A cry went up when they found him.

"Pike! Where've you been, for God's sake?"

The man was dishevelled and filthy. His hair was unkempt and he looked as if he had been sleeping rough. He dropped his bow.

"What's all this about Pike?" yelled Bennet, coming forward, "What is your quarrel with Basketwright?"

"You here astrologer? You have several lives like a cat I think."

All at once Bennet felt a menacing presence behind him and a body pressed up against his back.

"Do not move. Do not even breathe or it will be the last breath you take." The basket maker's sinister tones sounded in his ear.

Pike had meanwhile shaken off his discoverers and was swaggering up the bank.

"Basketwright! *There* you are. Thought I saw you in the crowd!" He was obviously drunk as he swayed about like the full udder of a goat.

"If I'd been sober, you would be dead now," he said.

Basketwright laughed. "You sober? That was never going to be."

"You saying you never touch a drop then?"

"If I wanted to kill a man, *I'd* make sure I *was* sober."

"You did all your best killin' drunk, by all accounts."

"What're you sayin', Pike?"

"Yer wife, yer mistress...God knows who else."

Still Basketwright didn't move and continued to use Bennet as a shield.

"What's your problem Pike?" cried the felon.

"You think I didn't know?"

Everyone was now silent listening to the argument between the basket maker and the blacksmith, not knowing how or whether to intervene.

"Know what?"

"Know that you and my wife were playing the two backed beast... behind my back."

"What if we were?"

"She said you were a drunkard...that you liked to play rough..."

"I didn't hear her complaining to me," said Basketwright.

"She confessed it to *me*."

"Good for her."

"Just before she died."

Christa saw Bennet look suddenly down at the ground as if a wave of guilt had passed over him.

"Aw...that's sad," said the basket maker with not a tinge of melancholy, sympathy nor regret.

"And so, I've come for you...basket maker." The blacksmith came closer. He turned his eye on Bennet.

"I wouldn't use him as a shield if I were you. I've come for him too. I don't care if he gets hurt."

Christa took in a frightened breath.

"Leave him alone," she yelled.

Pike turned a red eye on her. "Aw the little servant girl!"

He advanced closer to the party at the bridge's end.

"You get in the way girl...I can't be responsible for what 'appens." He took out a long knife.

The crowd gasped and glowered at the blacksmith but no one moved. Everyone was fearful of intervening.

Jonas Pike, Christa noticed, was now crying noiselessly; his cheeks were wet.

"He killed her as sure as he stuck a knife in her. And you...you lied to me," said Pike pointing a wavering finger at Bennet.

"Pike! Do you really want to shout this to the crowd? Let your wife rest in peace," said Bennet. "It cannot be proven that she killed herself. It was a terrible accident. The coroner said so."

"Ah no...I know what she did. I know the truth."

"Pike... let it be."

"Ah no. Don't you tell me to let it go. You're to blame too."

"And so you tried to blame the murder of the woman Jehanne Ferrers, upon Master Celest, in revenge?" cried Christa.

"He should've hanged for it."

"Hanged for a crime he didn't commit?" she yelled. "That's

230

despicable, Pike."

Bennet moderated his voice. "Come Jonas. Let's talk about this like sensible people."

Without a further word the blacksmith made a lunge and the basket weaver side stepped and took Bennet with him.

At that same moment the dog, who was still loose among the crowd leapt up and with two paws pushed Basketwright, who had not seen him approaching, in the back. He staggered off balance.

Bennet fell to his knees and then unable to right himself immediately, he tumbled down the slope and into the river.

He was rapidly followed by Basketwright who had been impaled upon the naked blade held out by Pike.

The basket maker, with gritted teeth and a mouth filling with blood, grabbed the blacksmith angrily by his arms and, turning in an arc, slowly fell into the waters by the bridge, taking Pike with him.

Christa shrieked and tried to follow to rescue Bennet, but was held back by strong hands.

She watched aghast as Master Milling threw off his cotte and leapt into the water after the other three men in order to rescue Bennet.

The water by the castle bridge was the deepest part of the river in the town. The flow was fast where it eddied around the starlings of the bridge. And the river was full, for it had been a rainy autumn and winter. There was a great deal of thrashing about and the waters boiled like vat of mash.

The figures had disappeared to the bottom of the river and all the onlookers held their breath as Master Milling, coming up for air, circled and once more dived into the yeasty froth.

"Oh Bennet," cried Christa into the breast of the priest, Father Torold, who had come up to mediate in the quarrel but who'd arrived an instant too late.

Men looked at each other in confusion.

One or two others threw off their clothes then, and leapt into the pool by the bridge, diving again and again to recover if not the live men, then the bodies.

Christa fell to the earth of the bank and began to weep into her hands. "Oh Bennet."

Just when she thought that he was surely lost, there was a sloshing noise and the sound of water running from a body.

Bennet Celest grabbing a tuft of grass dragged himself to the edge of the river, and gasping crawled up the bank. Helpful hands pulled him up and he turned over on his back and retched and coughed and panted like an old dray horse.

Christa threw herself onto him and half crying, half laughing she wrapped her arms around him until she became very wet herself.

After a while the search party abandoned their hunt and came up coughing and spluttering and shaking their heads.

"All muddied down there," said Harry Glazer with a stertorous breath, as someone threw a blanket over his back. "The whole river bed has been churned up and there are some dangerous underwater weeds just by the bridge."

Christa looked out over the water "Benedict!" she cried..."Oh no... Benedict!"

*****

Benedict Milling's body was recovered a few hours later. He had a large wound to his head which had either killed him, or rendered him unconscious, so that he took in water to his lungs and drowned. Christa gave a sobbing breath when she heard. "Oh he should have had a wren's feather about him. That would have protected him," she said.

The doctor looked at him and pronounced that he had probably fallen foul of the large underwater stones which made up the base of the stone bridge for he'd jumped in close to them to begin searching around.

The basket maker and the blacksmith were found the next day

downstream from the bridge, washed up by the culverstones behind the town mill, lying close to each other.

Each had a fatal wound to the chest.

Bennet and Christa admitted the town reeve to the house that following day, in company with Harry Glazer.

"I am sorry about Master Milling," said Nicholas. "He was a fine man. A good miller and a fine man and no doubt would have made an outstanding husband. My sincere condolences for your loss, Mistress Christa."

Christa chewed her lip.

Harry clapped Bennet on the back. "So glad to see you have come out of this with no great injury, Ben," he said.

"Ah…" Bennet put a hand to a large bruise on his forehead. "It's nothing. There are many submerged stones there. I think that must be what caught poor Ben Milling."

"That's what the doctor thinks," said Nicholas. "And the other two, well, it seems they continued to fight underwater and neither came off well."

Harry smiled a sad sort of smile. "This will be a Wren Day, the year of which will go down in Marlborough history."

"Aye it will," said the town reeve. "Erm…incidentally what was all that about Pike's wife? I hear from onlookers that he was blaming you for her death."

"Ah no, sir…not her death. Not exactly. It's a matter which arose from one of my consultations and, just as the priest has his seal of the confessional, then I have mine."

Nicholas looked slyly at Bennet. "Ah…convenient eh?"

"I too took an oath, sir, as does a priest and a doctor."

When they had gone, Bennet sat down and put his head in his hands, his elbows on his work table.

Christa came up and reached for his wrist.

"You may have the seal of the confessional like a priest but you will tell me, won't you? What happened with Pike?"

He looked deeply into her beautiful hazel eyes. How had he not truly realised just how beautiful they were?

"If I tell you…"

"I will never repeat it to a soul."

Bennet took in a deep and sad breath.

"Enyd Pike had been carrying on an extra marital relationship…"

"With my old master?"

"As it turns out…yes, though I didn't know who it was at the time. He wasn't the first, nor the only one."

"You knew she was adulterous because…?"

"I had cast her chart; her husband had asked me to do it."

"You didn't tell him that…" said Christa shocked.

"No, of course not. But I did tell her to *confess* it to her husband. Pike came to see me and tried to get the truth out of me but I wouldn't tell…I think he guessed."

"And eventually she confessed?"

"She did."

"Oh the poor woman. And so because she could not live with her sin, she…"

"Took her own life, yes."

"Oh no. How did she…do it?"

"She went the same way as her husband in the end. In the river. From the bridge."

"And you knew all this?"

"I cast her chart. I knew her state of mind but…I did not tell anyone that it was *felo de se*"

"Self murder."

"No, because if I *had* then the poor woman would not now be lying in the churchyard at St. Mary's.

"Oh…"

"She would be lying in a grave at the crossroads at the London Road, with a stake through her heart to stop her from walking in death."

"Oh no...that's awful. That is why you didn't want Pike to shout it out to everyone? That is why you stopped him."

"I would not like to think of her..."

"No, neither would I," said Christa with a sad gulp. "Why did Pike want to get even with you?"

"He had always known that Enyd was a woman of...if not exactly sexually promiscuous ways, then loose morals. She had been this way before they married. But he so loved her, he married her anyway. When I cast her chart, I did not know that it would show her infidelity and so I hid the fact from him, as I said."

"To save him great mortification."

"That and the censure of the town. They would all know that he was a cuckold."

"Oh and that he would never stomach. Not a man like him."

"No."

"And so he blamed you for not telling him the truth."

"Yes."

"Even though it had saved him from town gossip and his wife from an ignominious burial?"

"I did not think he would take it so far though. I had no idea that he would try to frame me for the deaths of Kydd and Ferrers in revenge. He was not in his right mind."

"Excess of drink does that," said Christa sadly.

Bennet's head went back into his hands. "Sometimes my job is a very...unhappy one."

Christa stroked his back.

"You were not to blame. You are a very sensitive man and only think to do the best for people, even if sometimes you are a little... misguided."

"I am sorry about your Master Milling, Christa. You must be feeling very sad about him and here's me going on about my own difficulties."

"Why does everyone assume he is *my* Master Milling?"

"Why? Was he not... erm... special to you?"

"He was a good friend, that's all. He wanted more from me than I could give him."

"But you do mourn his death."

Christa drew away from Bennet. "Of course I do but not as much as I would have mourned yours."

Bennet blinked.

"If it had been you I'd lost, I would now be lying on the floor weeping inconsolably, unable to speak."

Bennet swallowed. "Oh."

"And not because I am simply a servant and would then be masterless and have no roof over my head again."

"Oh."

"But because I could not imagine life without you, Bennet Celest, master astrologer."

Bennet stood and walked to the window, his heart pounding in his breast. He couldn't look at her for he knew that he would have leapt over and taken her in his arms and he was afraid to frighten her, as he was sure that such a grand show of affection would do.

"We have never been to Master Barbflet and had an agreement written between us, have we?"

"Hmmm?"

"To say that I am your master and you my servant."

Christa averted her eyes. This was not what she wanted to hear. "No."

"Well then, perhaps we should go and make our intentions known. If anything happens to me, I want you to be safe. Safe in the knowledge that this house will be yours and all that is in it and all that I have."

"What?"

"We need an agreement between us."

Christa stood stock still by the window, her mouth open in surprise.

"Perhaps we should go up to Father Torold and arrange for a

time for us to be married?"

Still Christa stood rooted to the spot.

"And there's no time like the present."

"What...?" A warm glow began to envelop Christa's heart. "What? You want me to marry you?"

"Well, if you are living with me here in this house and are not my servant, then you had better become my wife. Or people will talk." He smiled teasingly at her.

"Oh Bennet!"

She flew across the room and rushed into his embrace. Bennet dropped his chin and he kissed her lovingly on the lips.

Now, with *this* first kiss, she knew without doubt, what all the girls had been talking about.

*****

That night, lying together in the big bed where Bennet's master had lain nocturnally for most of his life and which Christa had used since she came to the house, they gave themselves wholly, as the legend of Tristan and Ysolde had said, to love.

Eventually Bennet took out the black book and turned to the last page.

"Let us read the book together...no secrets."

He turned his way through the pages. The day after St. Stephen's Day 1207.

'If the heavens have been kind and I have been correct in my prognostications, you Bennet should now be free of all danger, having realised the true nature of who you are. There will be no celibate life for you. Embrace your little wren and live a good life.'

"He knew all along, the wily..."

"What does he write here?' said Christa struggling with the meagre light of the bedside candle.

'Give yourself to good works in the town. Become a town

councillor as I should have done but never did. One day, you will be town reeve. I make this a prophecy."

"Oh," said Christa with disappointment, "does he not say how many children we shall have? I would like to know that."

She craned her neck to the lines on the page.

""Er no...but it does say..."

"What... what?" Her hazel eyes reflected the light from the candle.

"That you shall have a beautiful new kirtle of lavender in which to be married. That it will be *made* for you so that you will never have to make another garment for yourself...unless you wish it. And that you will look beautiful in it."

"No...it doesn't say that...does it?"

Bennet pulled her down laughing and the book fell to the floor.

His lips searching for hers, he said. "No, it just says that we shall be very, very happy."

And all night long, from the branch of Master Weaver's pear tree outside the window, the robin sang his chirruping nocturnal song.

The wren was nowhere to be seen.

❧ FIN ❧

GLOSSARY

Ampulla - a receptacle for holy water which was thought to have thaumatergic (magical) properties ie: the capability to work magic or other paranormal events or a saint to perform miracles.

Armillary Sphere - Three dimensional depiction of the heavens consisting of a spherical framework of rings, centred on the Earth or the Sun, that represent lines of celestial longitude and latitude and other astronomically important features.

Astrolabe - Type of early scientific instrument used for reckoning time and for observational purposes. One widely employed variety, the planispheric astrolabe, enabled astronomers to calculate the position of the Sun and prominent stars with respect to both the horizon and the meridian.

Barbette - Women's costume. A linen band which goes under the chin.

Braies - Underpants worn by men.

Brazier - A container used to burn charcoal or other solid fuel for cooking and heating.

Chamber Stick - A type of candle holder that has been designed for carrying.

Chandler - Maker of candles

Cist - Chest or coffer.

Cordwainer - Shoemaker.

Cotte - Long tunic worn by men or women.

Crespinette - A hairnet

Cunning Woman - A primitive doctor and healer who used charms and herbs to help those who, maybe couldn't afford a doctor.

Dun - Dull coloured, brown.

Fleshmonger - Seller of meat. Butcher.

Frith Chair/Stool - A seat, chair, or place of peace. Also OE frithstól, a place of sanctuary or safekeeping.

Goodmother - Mother in Law.

Goodpeople - Fairy folk.

Hue and Cry - A common law process where bystanders are summoned to help apprehend a criminal.

Jongleur - An itinerant minstrel.

Kalends - The first day of the month in the ancient Roman calendar.

Kirtle - Dress.

Matins - A series of prayers for the time at and after midnight.

Nightjar - A nocturnal bird.

Philtre - A drink supposed to arouse love and desire for a particular person in the drinker; a love potion.

Quarterstaff/longstaff - Staff being made from hardwood of a tree split or sawed into quarters.

St. Stephen's Day - 26th December.

Stylus - A pointed instrument for writing, marking, or incising such as used in writing on clay or waxed tablets.

Terce - The third hour of the day usually about 9 am.

Town Reeve - The town mayor.

Trull - Whore.

Vespers - The sixth of the canonical hours that is said or sung in the late afternoon. A service of evening worship.

Vigils - A religious service held during the night leading to a Sunday or other feast day.

SUSANNA M. NEWSTEAD

AUTHOR'S NOTE

Astrologers were a large part of Mediaeval life and many people consulted them for exactly the reasons I have stated in this book. I cannot truly say if small towns like Marlborough would have had a resident astrologer but you must indulge me.

A modern astrologer will say that it's not possible to be so accurate nor so specific in prognostications. True, I'm sure, if indeed you believe in it at all. Mediaeval man certainly did. I think that Bennet's master, Geoffrey was not only a superlative astrologer but perhaps a little psychic too. For the purposes of the story, I have made him be able to perfectly predict what was happening in Bennet's life, day to day.

Town reeves were those men who stood at the head of the town council, made up of influential men of the town; merchants, artisans, and wealthy men. Eventually they would morph into the mayor, the rest to town councillors.

We know that there was no effective police force in the 13th century. Towns were responsible for policing themselves, under the town council and the coroner, (sometimes known as the Crowner; the man appointed by the Crown to deal with unexpected deaths. The coroner was the man who drew up the jury of twelve men to decide the cause of death and if need be, impose fines,) sheriff (shire reeve) and other officers. The hue and cry was, in former English law, the cry raised by the inhabitants of a hundred (a measurement of land) in which a robbery or other crime had been committed, if they were not to become liable for the damages suffered by the victim.

Felo de se (suicide) was a sin for much of our history and those who committed it could not be buried in consecrated ground. It was feared that their shades would walk. Their souls would never enter Heaven.

The river in Marlborough was a lot deeper in the 13th century in certain places than it is today. Now, water is taken from the Kennet by the water authorities and this depletes the depth. Change in rainfall is another contributing factor.

Some readers of The Savernake Novels will recognise characters from the series, appearing in this book; the doctor Johannes of Salerno, Harry Glazer and the Town Reeve, Nicholas Barbflet amongst others.

Go to: susannamnewstead.co.uk for more information.

Please be aware that knowledge of the celestial bodies was different in the 13th century. Now we know that the earth revolves around the sun but in the past and until the 17th century, it was thought that the sun moved. There were also only seven known planets, Jupiter, Mercury, Venus, Mars, Saturn and the two luminaries, the moon and the sun. Pluto and Uranus were later discoveries. There were no telescopes at the time about which I write.

ABOUT THE AUTHOR

Susanna has known the area around Marlborough all her life. After a period at the University of Wales studying Speech Therapy, she returned to Wiltshire where she soaked up the abundant history of the area, particularly that of the 12th and 13th centuries, and began to write about it in her twenties. She now lives in Northamptonshire with her husband and two small wire haired fox terriers called Delphi and Tabor. Forty years of writing Mediaeval murder mysteries and now we have number two in the romance series. Susanna hopes to return fairly soon to her beloved Wiltshire downs where she will continue to write the Savernake series and her romances set in the area around Marlborough, Wiltshire.

ALSO BY SUSANNA M. NEWSTEAD

The Savernake Medieval Murder Mysteries

Belvoir's Promise
She Moved Through the Fair
Down by the Salley Gardens
I Will Give my Love an Apple
Black is the Colour of my True Love's Hair
Long Lankyn
One Misty Moisty Morning
The Unquiet Grave
The Lark in the Morning
A Parcel of Rogues
Bushes & Briars

Illustrated Children's Books

Tabor the Terrierble: The Gardner's Dog
Tabor the Terrierble: The Dark Knight

Please visit her website for further information
https://susannamnewstead.co.uk/

Lightning Source UK Ltd.
Milton Keynes UK
UKHW010658030621
384853UK00002B/64